Sea of Trees

Wolfie Smoke

To:
Cody,
To inspire you

1 Peter 3:8

Finally, all of you, have unity of mind, sympathy, brotherly love, a tender heart, and a humble mind.

Sea of Trees

By Wolfie Smoke

Contents

Chapter 1
Nat

It was almost four o'clock as Nat walked home from school. He passed the church, the store, and some apartment buildings along the dirt road. His sandals left prints behind him.

Nat lived in a small town called Nesserad, he was ten years old, tall, skinny, had red hair, bright blue eyes, and his pale skin was covered in freckles.

"Hey, Nat!" Samuel, Nat's best friend, came running up next to him.

"What?" asked Nat, Samuel always had some new thing to tell.

Samuel was Nat's age but was a head taller than Nat. He had very dark skin, and brown hair, almost black, and lighter brown eyes.

"Gus and me found a patch of clovers over near the old well. After dinner we're gonna look for some four leaf ones! Wanna help?"

Nat smiled, "I'll meet you there!"

"Great! Gotta go, see you then."

Samuel sped off; he was always in a hurry.

Nat went on his way along the road, he was taking the long way home, that way he would pass his favorite shop, Will's Weapons.

When he entered the store, Nat was welcomed by Will's voice.

"There's my favorite customer!" he said.

"Hi, Will," Nat said, eyes already scanning the row of new knives and daggers.

Nat's gaze fell upon a dagger with double sided blade and a sky blue handle.

Will followed Nat's gaze. "I knew that dagger would catch your attention," he said.

Will was big; Sometimes Nat heard younger kids call him a giant. He was bald and had a short beard, his skin had a gray tint, he had shiny teal eyes and large earlobes.

"How much is it?" Nat asked hopefully.

"Five gold pieces."

Nat gave him the money happily.

"By the way Nat, do you know of anyone looking for a job?" asked Will.

"No. Why?"

"Well, it's getting a little hard running this place by myself, so if you see anyone looking for a job you send them over here. Ok?"

"Ok." Nat went over and took the blade off the shelf.

"Would you like to have the scabbard too?" Will asked.

"How much?"

"For you, free."

"Really?!"

"Yeah, after all, you are my best customer."

Will gave Nat the scabbard, sky blue like the handle.

"Thanks Will!" Nat went out the door and continued his way home.

The sky was slowly changing from a blue it shared with the scabbard to a dark, swirly pink, followed by a royal purple.

Nat walked up to his front door. He saw lights in the windows. His dad must have gotten back from the hotel early.

Nat's dad worked as a manager in a hotel around the corner. Nat had been there once, but he had never stayed there, or in any hotel.

Nat let himself in. Their house wasn't much different than the average Nesserad home. Main floor with a den, kitchen, dining room, etcetera. They had a second floor where the bedrooms were and a rarely entered basement.

Nat's dad was in the kitchen, standing over a pot of soup.

"Hi, Nat," said his dad, "how was school?"

That was one of the typical questions from his dad, but Nat loved answering his typical questions.

"Today was debate day," Nat sat at the wooden kitchen table.

"Ah. Did you get to debate?" His dad was staring into the red soup he was stirring with a wooden spoon.

Nat's dad had no hair, but if he did it would be red like Nat's. He had blue eyes, but it was a lighter blue than Nat's, almost the color of Nat's scabbard. He was tall and skinny like Nat, but he had no freckles. He might of had them when he was younger but he had none now.

"Yes," Nat answered his dad's question, "The debate was about how they should handle the money in Bork."

"Ahh, Bork is a beautiful place," his dad said, almost sadly.

Nat's dad was into travel, but he hadn't been able to arrange it since before Nat was born. Nat was secretly thankful for that, he didn't think travel would be fun. What was wrong with Nesserad?

Nat and his dad had lived in the same house for as long as Nat could remember. He had never been outside of Nesserad, and he was okay with that.

"So who did you debate against?" asked Nat's dad.

"Aric," Nat said grimly.

Aric was Nat's age but Nat didn't like him at all. Aric had won the debate, as well as the short story contest Nat had entered.

"Aric. Isn't that the new kid in your class?"

"Yes. What's for dinner?" Nat wanted the subject to change from Aric.

"Tomato soup and mashed potatoes."

After dinner Nat rushed up to his bedroom. His room wasn't small or big, but he loved it. His room held his bed, his dresser, a small bay window looking out onto the street and a shelf holding three shoe boxes where he kept his knife collection.

The knife collection was where Nat kept all the daggers and knives he'd gotten over the years. There were new knives, old daggers, double blades, jagged blades, ones with fancy designs on the handles, and a majority of other shapes and colors.

Once Will had an amazing dagger, its red handle was jewel encrusted, but what Nat had really liked about it was the blade.

The blade was zigzagged, shaped like lightning. Nat had never seen a dagger like it. He would of bought it, but it was way too expensive.

Nat added his new dagger to his collection. Now, should he bring anything with him to the clover patch? He looked around. His untouched journal sat on his nightstand, next to a sharp pencil.

A friend of Nat's, Cynthia, had given it to him on his ninth birthday; he hadn't found a use for it yet. Why not take it now?

Nat emptied his backpack of all his school stuff and dropped in the leather journal, and the pencil. Why bring the journal and not the pencil?

Nat added a magnifying glass to his pack, sped downstairs, said bye to his dad, and sprinted out the door toward the old abandoned well.

Chapter 2
Aric

Somewhere in a different part of Nesserad ten year old Aric sat on the steps of the school building, writing on some scrap paper that Jason, a volunteer at Aric's orphanage, had given him.

Aric looked nothing like Nat. Aric had tan skin, black hair, pronounced eyebrows, and chocolate brown eyes, he wasn't exactly fat, but he was definitely not skinny.

Aric looked up from his writing. He loved to run, but not to the orphanage where he now lived.

He used to live in a big city before his parents drowned in a flood, he had lived in the orphanage in his hometown before it ran out of money, which was when he was transferred here.

Aric didn't much like Nesserad. Nesserad was pretty much in the middle of nowhere. In all directions, north, south, east, and west were miles of woods.

You couldn't blame him; he had lived in big cities surrounded by bigger cities all his life and he had just been sent to Nesserad last month. He had tried in failure to fit in and make friends.

Aric thought of Nesserad as an island in the middle of a sea of trees.

Aric went back to his writing. On a blank, crumpled piece of paper he wrote:

I'm now sitting on the steps of the school; I'm in no hurry to get back to the orphanage.

During school I won the debate but I'm convinced that the teacher gave me the win out of pity. I think Nat did better than me.

I don't think Nat likes me, he more than just ignores me like everyone else but he keeps glaring at me and he sometimes calls me names...

Aric ran out of room and flipped to the other side of the paper.

I don't know why he's mad at me. I should be mad at him for being mad at me! After all he has friends, I don't. He's athletic and strong, I'm not. That was confirmed yesterday when he made the track team and I didn't. I wonder if I should consider him an enemy? He seems to think I'm his enemy for some reason...

The crumpled paper was now full so Aric swapped it with another piece from his backpack.

Before he could write more the clock tower's bells announced six o'clock, Aric was already late and he would probably get a small scalding from Jason, nevertheless Aric wrote one more sentence before heading to the orphanage:

He has a dad, I don't.

Jason was sitting on the steps when Aric finally reached the orphanage.

"Where were you?" he asked in a stern but somehow soft voice.

Jason's skin was pretty tan but not as much as Aric's. He was seventeen years old, had soft brown hair and green eyes. He was tall and skinny, probably the shape Nat would have when he was older.

"School," Aric answered.

"You can't stay out this late Aric, it's almost dark."

"I know," Aric said bitterly.

"Come on, you have to eat your dinner."

Dinner was mostly just bread and butter. Aric sat at the dining room table, meant for ten, next to Jason.

No one else was at the table, Aric was the only orphan in Nesserad, the few friends he had from the last orphanage had been adopted or sent to foster homes.

"After dinner I need you to run to the store for me," said Jason.

"Ok," said Aric. He had learned not to argue, even if it was almost dark out.

Chapter 3
Kidnapped

Nat could see the old well as he approached it.
The old well was a popular landmark for the kids of Nesserad, there were others in the small town, the well was just one. It was not, however, a good place to get water. It had dried up long before Nat was born.

As the royal purple sky darkened to a deep navy blue, Nat could make out the crumbling stone and rotting wood of the well. The vines that clung to it and the tall grass and large clover patches that surrounded it would have been cut away long ago if the well was still in use.

Samuel and Gus were already there on their hands and knees, running their fingers through different patches of clover.

"Did you find any yet?" asked Nat.

"No," said Gus. Gus had short blonde hair, a chubby figure, and a pudgy face.

"Not yet," agreed Samuel.

Nat got on his hands and knees and looked through a patch of clovers. After a while he started on another patch.

He made his way to a patch next to the woods He was about to pull out his magnifying glass before a clammy hand covered his mouth.

Aric entered the store, out of breath from running there.

The store was lit with pale, dim light.

Aric looked down at the list in his hand:

Apples

Ham

Plates

Blankets

Mints

Pencils & Paper

Aric fiddled with the bit of gold and silver Jason had given him to pay for the stuff.

Aric grabbed a shopping basket and started looking for the candy aisle.

As he entered the candy aisle his mind recalled memories of him and his old friends sharing candy. He wished he had at least one friend, but no one ever seemed to want to talk to him.

Aric dropped a bag of green mints into the basket and started to the linens aisle to get the blankets.

Like the candy aisle, the linens aisle placed sad thoughts into Aric's head, not about friends, but about the future.

Aric didn't think he had much of a future, not now that he lived in an orphanage in a small town in the middle of nowhere.

Aric had hoped of becoming a writer, when his parents were alive they had given him journal after journal. Sometimes he stayed up all night writing and would fill a journal in less than a week.

Aric wished he could have a journal, but all his had been swept away in the flood.

Aric put two soft blankets into the shopping basket and made his way to the food aisle.

As Aric searched for apples and canned ham his mind settled on the debate that day. He was absolutely sure that the teacher had declared him the winner out of pity. He hadn't thought so at first, but after he thought about it, Nat had definitely given a better argument.

Aric wished he could be as good as Nat, not just at debate but everything. Nat had won the debate because he was smart, and he had the spot on the track team because he was athletic, and he had friends because he wasn't the new kid no one wants to talk to.

He grabbed a bag of apples and started looking over the canned ham as he thought about Nat. Why did Nat hate him? The thought made Aric hate Nat. What was it about him that made Nat hate him?

Aric walked over to the school supplies aisle and stopped.

Cynthia was there looking at the different journals. Aric hid in the next aisle before she could see him.

Cynthia had deep blue eyes, a small nose, and long, mousy blonde hair that she usually wore in a ponytail.

Aric always got nervous around her. If her friends weren't around she might talk to him. Aric understood, he didn't like standing out either, but he wished she would talk to him. In his opinion she was very pretty.

Aric peeked around the corner, Cynthia was still there, he decided to get the plates while he waited for her to leave.

The butter knives next to the plates reminded Aric of a dagger he had in his backpack. It had been his dad's dagger; it was the only thing that had survived the flood besides Aric.

To anyone else a thing that got passed down to you from your dead parents would be a good thing, especially if it was the only thing you had of theirs, but to Aric it was just a reminder that they were dead. Aric would have gotten rid of it a long time ago had it not seemed wrong. Aric didn't need the dagger; he had hundreds of memories to help remember his parents.

Aric grabbed the plates and went back to the school supplies aisle. Cynthia was gone. He sighed with equal relief and disappointment, grabbed the paper and a pack of sharpened pencils, and went up to a cashier.

Aric handed the basket to the cashier, who looked through the items and added the price in his head, after awhile he said: "fifteen gold pieces and one silver piece."

Aric counted out the money, placed it on the counter, put the items in his backpack and went out the door.

It was a beautiful, breezy night, peaceful too, at least it seemed that way.

A hand clapped over Aric's mouth, he tried to scream, but the hand muted him. He tried to scramble away, but someone's hand had a firm grip on his arm.

Aric was dragged into the woods before he knew it.

In the woods the man pulled Aric towards a gang of men all dressed in boots, gloves, and dark robes with hoods that covered their faces.

"I got one more," the kidnapper holding Aric said in a deep voice.

"Good, you know where to put him," said another kidnapper in a voice so deep Aric couldn't hardly understand him, "that should be enough."

The man gagged Aric with a piece of cloth and tied his hands behind his back with rough rope before dragging him deeper into the woods.

Aric looked over his shoulder, he couldn't see the lights of Nesserad.

The small amount of moonlight wasn't enough for Aric to see in the dark, but the kidnapper seemed to be able to see very well as he swept through the woods.

They came to an old dirt road that looked like it hadn't been traveled in years. It was so overgrown you could hardly see it under the vines, grass, dead leaves, and the occasional mushroom.

As they neared it, Aric could make out a horse drawn buggy. He saw that other kids, bound and gagged like him, were in it. Some quiet, some trying to escape. A kidnapper stood guard over them.

Aric was placed in the buggy with the others; he thought some of the kids looked familiar.

A familiar sniffle told Aric that a terrified Cynthia was near the front of the buggy. She must have been grabbed outside the store like Aric.

On top of his fear for himself, Aric felt a pang of anger that they had kidnapped Cynthia too.

Across from Cynthia was a pudgy face, which was a tell-tale sign of someone he knew. It was Gus.

Gus seemed pretty scared too, but no one could have more fear than Cynthia at that moment.

It looked like Samuel was next to Gus, and who was that next to Samuel? Nat? Aric couldn't tell in the darkening darkness.

Chapter 4
Loose Rope

Nat did a good job of looking brave, but of course he was scared, he had never been this far from Nesserad. He'd never been outside of Nesserad at all! All the summer vacations and spring breaks had been spent at home. It was terrifying!

Nat remembered his dad telling him that he and Nat's mom had gone on hundreds of trips up mountains and through cities. When Nat was born they still tried to go on trips, but there was never a good time. Then Nat's mom got sick and died.

Nat's dad had tried to plan trips after that, but it never happened.

Nat looked up at the sky, the half moon was almost directly above his head. *It must be around midnight,* thought Nat. *wasn't it around eight when we were taken?*

It didn't feel like the buggy had been going for hours, but it must have been.

They had started off not long after they were caught. Nat wondered how far they were from Nesserad, probably miles and miles away.

Nat felt a nudge on his shoulder; he looked at Samuel who had somehow been able to lose his gag.

"Nat," he whispered, "your hands aren't tied very good. If you turn a little I can untie you and you could go get help!"

It sounded like a good idea, Nat didn't want to leave his friends behind, but if he tried to untie them all the kidnappers would notice and would put a stop to it.

Nat looked around at his sleeping schoolmates. The kidnappers on the cart had their attention on the road ahead.

Nat turned his back to Samuel, and soon Nat felt Samuel using the fingers sticking out from his ropes to free his arms.

Nat pulled his hands apart and pulled down his gag.

"Go!" hissed Samuel.

As Nat stood up he realized that he was still wearing his backpack. He took one more look at his friends and jumped over the side of the buggy.

"Did you hear a noise?" one kidnapper asked another.

"What noise?" asked the other kidnapper.

"It sounded like a big thud, like a sandbag dropping."

"It was probably nothing."

"Yeah, you're probably right."

Nat ran in the direction he hoped was the way home. He had decided to go through the woods instead of the road. If the kidnappers realized he was missing, they would look for him along the road. He was safer in the woods. Probably.

Nat was very tired but he kept running through the dark woods. All his schoolmates were depending on him to get… somewhere, hopefully home, so he could get help.

Nat finally decided to rest. He sat on a patch of moss, his back against a tree trunk.

He planned to just stay there for a second, just long enough to catch his breath.

Nat looked around. It would be pitch black if it weren't for dim rays of moonlight that managed to escape the clutches of the overhanging leaves and branches.

A cloud covered the moon. Unwillingly, Nat felt his eyes shut. He fell asleep.

Chapter 5
Lost With Your
Enemy

When Nat woke he was surprised to see Aric standing over him.

Nat sat up straight, "Aric?!"

"Nat?"

"How... why… how did you get here?!"

"The kidnappers got me and I fell out of their buggy."

Nat's back hurt from leaning back on his backpack, he noticed Aric wore his too.

The woods were definitely brighter in the day, but it was still pretty dark, at least they could see. A bird chirped somewhere in the distance.

Nat stood up, "How did you get out of your ropes?" he asked accusingly.

"I could ask you the same question!" answered Aric defensively.

"I asked you first!"

"Fine!" snapped Aric, "I found a sharp rock and cut the rope with it! Now you."

"Samuel undid my ropes for me," said Nat, beginning to feel calmer.

"Did you jump off the buggy?" asked Aric, also sounding calmer.

"Yes."

Neither of the boys spoke for a minute. Nat didn't think Aric liked him much more than Nat liked him.

"Shouldn't we get help or something?" asked Aric.

"Yes," said Nat.

"Let's call a truce," Aric said randomly and suddenly. He held out his hand.

Nat looked at Aric, it wasn't like they were official enemies, they never actually got into a fight, but he guessed he had been meaner to Aric than necessary.

Nat took Aric's hand and gave a small shake.

"Truce," agreed Nat.

"So which way back to Nesserad?" Aric asked, as if he thought Nat had everything figured out.

Which way was Nat going last night? He looked around. He felt like he was in a completely different part of the woods than where he fell asleep.

"I don't know," Nat admitted.

Aric looked surprised. "But you've lived around here for a long time!"

"Not this far out," said Nat, "I've never been out in these woods."

"Haven't you ever gone camping here before?"

"No, I've never been camping at all." Nat started looking around for anything he recognized from the night before. He laid down his backpack.

"Then what do you do all summer?" asked Aric.

"Stay home," said Nat, "We never go on trips."

Aric was quiet for a second. When his parents were alive they never missed a summer trip.

Whether it was go to the beach, camping, staying in a fancy resort, they always did something. Not once did Aric remember being home the whole summer.

It seemed crazy to him that Nat had never been outside of Nesserad. To him it would be like prison.

Nat walked over to a big pile of large rocks.

"So you stay home the whole summer? Every summer?" asked Aric

"Yes." Nat started climbing the rock pile, hoping that being higher would help him see around, even though he would still be under the trees.

Aric watched Nat climb. He was halfway to the top.

Nat reached the top of the pile, all he could see was trees. *Why does it have to be spring?* Nat thought as he tried to see past the fresh, green leaves.

"Do you see anything?" Aric called up.

"No, just trees. Stupid spring!" Nat started his way down. "I guess we'll just have to go in a random direction and hope that we end up somewhere."

Nat decided he was close enough to jump the rest of the way; He hit the ground in front of Aric.

"Let's look through our bags and see if we have anything useful." Nat picked up his bag and sat on the ground. Aric did the same.

Aric's bag was crammed full and heavy. Nat's on the other hand looked almost empty.

Nat rummaged through his bag, he pulled stuff out as he named them.

"A pencil, a journal, and my magnifying glass." he said.

Nat didn't strike Aric as a journaler, but he had a journal, an empty one, Aric could tell by the way the pages were crisp, flat and clean. A used journal would have ruffled up pages. Aric would know, he had filed a million.

Nat was staring at Aric and Aric realized Nat was waiting for him to empty his backpack. Aric opened his backpack and started through it, bringing the stuff out as he named them the way Nat did.

"Let's see. A box of pencils, a bag of apples, three cans of ham, plates, a couple blankets, a bag of mints, scrap paper, and my math and history textbooks from school."

At least he had been kidnapped before he dropped the food back at the orphanage.

Aric looked into his backpack, he had gotten everything but the dagger.

"Is that it?" asked Nat.

"Yes," lied Aric. He liked to pretend that the dagger didn't exist, even though he knew it was deceitful to Nat.

Nat looked at Aric's stuff. "How many apples are in the bag?"

Aric counted, "Five," he said.

"Let's have one each, I'm starving!"

Aric took an apple and handed one to Nat. The boys put their things back in their packs before eating.

While Nat was eating he started wishing he had untied at least Samuel, but if he had tried he would have regretted it. The kidnappers would have seen him and tied him back up, but better, and he would still be on his way to...

Nat suddenly realized that he had no idea where the kidnappers were taking them. What was the point of getting help if he didn't know where they were going?!

Nat tossed his apple core into the trees, "Do you know where the kidnappers were going?" he asked Aric.

Aric was silent for a moment, "No," he said. He felt bad because he felt like he was supposed to know the answer, he didn't know why. It was like a bomb was about to go off and he was the last person to be asked if he knew how to defuse it.

Nat sighed, "How are we going to get help if we don't even know where they're going?"

Nat stood up and started pacing, as he paced Aric took scrap paper and a pencil and started writing:

There's not much we can do without knowing where they're going, even if we can get help we have no idea where to send it!

Aric stopped for a moment, then continued:

I hope Cynthia's ok. She doesn't seem like the kind of person who's good in a crisis. I'm sure Samuel's fine; he's good in a crisis. Last week he put out a small fire in school. Gus probably isn't as good; I don't think he's as tough as he acts.

Nat stopped pacing, "I guess there's nothing we can do except keep trying to find help."

Aric frowned. He didn't like most of those kids, except Cynthia, but he didn't want them to be kidnapped. He didn't want anyone to get kidnapped.

"I guess we'll just have to find our way home," said Nat, "or to some town, and hope someone will know what to do. Which way do you think home is?"

"I don't know, but the woods have to end somewhere, so we could just keep walking until we find someone who will help us."

"Ok, that sounds good, but which way do we go?"

"Well, which way were you going last night?" Aric didn't want to be the one who decided which way they went.

"I can't tell," said Nat.

"Rats!" Aric said under his breath.

"How about east?" asked Nat.

"Ok, which way's east?"

"I think it's that way," Nat pointed.

"Ok, we'll go that way, but first, can you carry the food in your backpack? Mine's really heavy."

After transferring the apples, ham, and mints into Nat's bag they started off towards east. At least, they thought it was east.

Chapter 6
Dust, Mildew, and Dirt

A slight breeze blew through the bright green leaves overhead. A bird chirped behind them, Aric tried to see it and stubbed his toe on a rock. Nat took no notice, of Aric or the bird.

Aric's toe didn't really hurt; the rock had a padding of moss on it.

The boys walked ankle deep in light green grass, the more they walked the darker the tree bark seemed to get and the more lush vines clutched to them.

Nat was doing his best to walk in a straight line. Aric on the other hand had his head high in the clouds.

Aric heard a faint buzzing noise along with a sweet smell.

"I think there are honey bees around here," he said.

"Aric, this is not the time to chase bees," Nat snapped.

What's his problem? Wondered Aric, *I'm only trying to make the best of things.*

Aric's pack was getting heavy, "I'm hungry," he said.

"We don't have much food Aric, we can only eat breakfast in the morning and dinner at night." Nat swatted a mosquito on his arm. Why weren't the bugs bothering Aric?

"Well, can we please take a break?" Aric begged.

"No, we have to get help as fast as we can," plus Nat wanted to get away from the woods and bugs; he was covered in itchy welts!

"How do we know that we're even headed for the nearest place?"

Nat stopped and faced Aric, "What do you mean?" he asked.

"I mean what if the nearest way out of these woods is that way," Aric pointed in the direction they were walking away from.

Nat started walking again in the same direction they were before, "We have to get somewhere eventually. Besides, what if the nearest town is the way we're going already?"

So they continued in the same direction for a few hours as Aric got hungrier and hungrier.

The sun was setting in a purple-orange sky. The birds had stopped chirping; in their place were cricket songs. By now Nat was getting hungry too.

"Are we going to stop and sleep eventually or are we going to walk all night long?" asked Aric.

Nat thought about it.

"It'll be too dark to see anyway," he said, "but let's walk a little longer and see if we can find a good place to eat and sleep."

After a while Aric saw something through the trees.

"Look!" he pointed.

Up ahead was a small wooden cabin that looked as if it wasn't used to being lived in. The wood looked dry and dead. Vines climbed up its walls and in and out of holes in the old windows.

As they got closer they saw a broken rocking chair on the front porch. A porch swing was on the other side; one rusty chain keeping it hung to the roof the other just as rusty, and broken too, leaving the swing tilted. When it broke, the swing made a big hole in the wood floor.

Nat, with Aric close behind him, walked up to a broken window on the side and looked in. It was too dark to see.

They made their way to another window, not broken, but so filthy they couldn't make much out, even so they could still tell it was a kitchen with a round, wooden table surrounded with four chairs, one of which was sideways on the floor, a stove with a disgusting looking fridge next to it, and a counter.

There weren't any tell-tale signs of people. No sound of footsteps, no pot of soup on the stove, no nothing.

The kitchen looked so dirty, but it might have been the gross glass.

"Should we go in?" asked Nat.

"What if someone lives here?" whispered Aric as if someone might hear him.

"If they do then maybe they could help us, but do you really think someone would live in a place like this?"

He had a point, "Ok," said Aric.

"After all, it's only for tonight. We leave first thing in the morning."

The boys walked around to the front.

"Ok," said Nat, "you go ahead and look around inside and I'll stay out here and figure out how to remember which way we were going."

Aric nodded his head and cautiously walked up the porch steps. He didn't want an injury due to wood rot.

Aric knocked on the door and called, "Hello!" just to be sure, after he was answered by silence he opened the door and went in.

The light was getting dimmer, the sun had set by now, not that the boys could tell through the trees. The orangeness had faded from the sky leaving the light blue-purple color disguised by a canopy of clouds that cast a grey tent on the earth.

Nat picked up a straight, rough stick that was still fresh, it must have fallen recently. He put his backpack on the ground and looked around. He saw another lush, Y-shaped stick and grabbed it.

Nat took the Y stick and shoved the bottom of the Y into the ground. He then took the long stick and wedged the middle into the fork in the upright Y-stick. One side of the stick touching the ground while the other pointed upwards like a see-saw. The side pointing up faced the direction they had been walking. This would be their way of knowing which way to go.

The cabin was very musty and dark on the inside. Aric walked into a small foyer, a coat stand leaned against the wall, a small shelf and a mirror in need of cleaning was on the opposite wall.

An old compass was on the shelf, Aric picked it up. It was very old and dusty but it looked like it still worked, it might be useful, but it belonged to someone. Or did it?

Aric debated with himself about whether to take it or leave it. Finally, he put the compass in his backpack, but left his math and history books in it's place. Probably no one wanted the compass, but leaving his schoolbooks made him feel better about taking it anyway, plus it was less weight in his pack.

Aric continued into what probably was a den. Maroon walls made the room seem darker than it already was, a red couch sat on one wall next to a matching arm chair in a corner, they were both ragged and torn and very dusty, a coffee table sat between them. Two small windows sat on either side of a crumbly, cold fireplace. One of them was broken; glass was on the floor beneath it.

Through a narrow door Aric went into the kitchen. It was much dirtier than it had looked through the window, which was stained green with mold both inside and out. The floor was covered in dirt and dust from where Aric stood to the back door, it even covered the counter.

Aric wiped his finger on the counter leaving a very clear line in the dust.

Some dark goo had stained the fridge; it went in a line from top to bottom right down the middle of the door. Aric opened it releasing a horrible rotten egg and expired milk smell, even though the fridge was empty.

Aric grabbed his nose, gagged, and closed the fridge. He turned his gaze to the stove, old fashioned like the fridge, and it also had dark goo down the sides.

Aric went through another door to a small hallway. There were two doors; the first of which Aric opened and found was a closet.

The closet was filled with unraveling blankets, moth eaten quilts and glass jars filled with old mayonnaise, peanut butter, fortunes from fortune cookies, buttons of all shapes and sizes, nuts, bottle caps, stamps, and even a jar with smaller jars in it.

Aric wondered if the nuts were still good as he analyzed a jar that was filled with what looked like money from another country. He decided they must be bad and closed the closet door.

The other door led to a small bedroom that looked lived in, by a pig. A pair of old boots were carelessly lying on the floor on opposite ends of the room, stained rags that might have been clothes at one point carpeted the floor, a not-very-stable-looking chair was on it's side next to an unmade bed, if you could call it a bed, it was really a mildewy mattress lying on the ground with a wrinkled army blanket on it. A small window did no help in lighting the room, mostly because it was dark out.

The house was now completely explored so Aric made his way back outside, Nat met him on the front porch.

"What do you think?" he gestured to his see-saw thing, "The side pointing up is facing the direction we're going."

"Great." said Aric.

"So, what did you find inside?"

"Dust, mildew, dirt, oh! And this." Aric pulled the compass out of his pack.

"Really!" said Nat, "That could be useful!" Nat took the compass and checked the direction they had been going in.

"We were headed east," said Nat as he put the compass in his backpack, "help me remember that."

"Ok," said Aric, "I will."

Chapter 7
A Little Crazy

Aric and Nat sat at the kitchen table. The daylight was almost completely gone.

Nat put his backpack on the table and pulled out the apples, ham and mints.

Finally! Thought Aric, *I'm starving!*

"We'll split a can of ham," said Nat, "Then we can each have a mint."

Aric agreed, even though he knew his stomach would want more than half a can of ham and a mint. He pulled out the plates from his pack.

By the time they finished their almost-meal, the only means of light outside was a not-quite-full moon. Luckily, Nat had found candles and matches in the kitchen drawers.

The boys went to the den and in the candlelight Aric pulled out the blankets from the store. He handed one to Nat and kept one for himself.

Nat laid his backpack on the ground and settled in the worn comfy chair. Aric spread out on the couch with his pack as a pillow. It wasn't very comfortable but it was better than nothing.

"Goodnight, Nat," Aric said.

"Goodnight," Nat said groggily.

The boys quickly fell asleep.

Nat didn't know how long he had slept, but he woke to the sound of a door opening and closing.

It was still dark out, even the crickets were asleep.

Nat thought the back door in the kitchen must have opened, but who opened it? Aric was right there on the couch, still asleep. Someone else must be in the house!

Nat held his breath. A still lit, now very short candle was on the coffee table, he had forgotten to blow it out before he fell asleep.

From the kitchen Nat heard footsteps, a raspy cough, and more footsteps, not coming closer but getting fainter. *He must be going to the bedroom,* Nat thought.

Nat heard a sound like metal scraping against the floor, whoever was in the cabin with them had some kind of tool, or maybe it was a weapon!

The sound of the bedroom door opening and closing came from the end of the hall. Then silence.

Nat quietly got up and shook Aric awake.

"What is it?" Aric groaned.

"Shh!" Nat whispered, "I think the owners are back!"

Aric was now fully awake and standing. "Who is it? What do we do?!" Aric asked in a shrill whisper, "We have to get out of here!" he answered his own question.

"Shh! I know, grab your backpack, we'll go out the front door."

The boys quietly picked up their backpacks and started tip-toeing to the front door.

"Wait!" whispered Aric, "What about our food? It's in the kitchen!"

"Well we can't leave our food behind!" Nat answered.

The boys tip-toed back into the kitchen. Nat was starting to get more worried; he had heard about hermits that live alone in the woods, he'd been told they were sometimes a little crazy.

While Nat was worrying about hermits he bumped into the table. It tipped over with a crash, the plates shattered on the floor, the ham and apples tumbled all over the place as if they were trying to make as much noise as possible.

Nat swooped down and grabbed the bag of apples, but he had grabbed it by the bottom letting all the apples spill out the top, only making more noise.

Just then a big, hairy, growling, angry looking man stepped out of the hall. He was definitely a hermit. His clothes were dirty, worn, and covered in holes. He had long, mousy brown hair with a matching beard, his snarl showed yellow teeth, and his grey animal like eyes glared at the boys, in his monster-like claws he held a dirty shovel.

The hermit didn't say anything, but he raised the shovel over his head like an ax.

The boys dodged to the back door just as the hermit brought the shovel down, smashing the sideways table in half.

Aric grabbed the brass doorknob. Locked. The hermit was blocking their way to the front door so Nat lead the way into the hall. They sped into the bedroom, Aric slammed the door, Nat barricaded it with the wooden chair.

Nat pointed at the window above the mattress, "Through there!" he yelled.

The hermit started banging on the door. The chair wouldn't hold long.

Nat climbed onto the bed and out the window, Aric quickly did the same.

As soon as Aric hit the ground the chair broke and the hermit crashed in. Luckily, the hermit was too big to get through the window so he started for the front door.

The boys were already running as fast as they could into the dark woods, the almost full moon just outlining the trees. The boys didn't know which way they were going, but at that moment they didn't care.

They ran for a good while and they were both good runners, but in different ways. Nat was faster and Aric kept his breath longer, and soon Nat was out of breath.

"St-stop!" Nat called, speaking between gasps. Aric stopped.

"I th-... I think we... I think we lost him," Nat managed to get out. He wiped his brow. It was very hot and humid in the woods, even at night.

The woods were strangely quiet; the hermit must have gotten tired of them. An owl hooted somewhere, breaking the silence.

Aric waited for Nat to catch his breath, and then asked, "What do we do now?"

"Let's check our stuff." Nat realized he was still clutching the empty apple bag.

He knelt on the ground and opened his backpack. He still had his magnifying glass, journal, and the compass, but all the food had been left at the cabin, even the mints, and it definitely wasn't an option to go back. He put the apple bag in his pack, just in case.

"All the food is with the hermit," Nat said to Aric, who was looking through his own backpack.

"We left the plates and blankets too," Aric groaned. All he had left were the pencils, paper, and, thanks to what he could only expect to be a curse, his dad's dagger.

The boys reported to each other what they did have, Aric left out the dagger though, even though he knew leaving it out probably wasn't a good idea.

"Let's find another place to sleep," said Nat.

It was too dark to see the compass so they walked in the opposite direction of the cabin in the straightest line they could walk.

They came to a river trickling quietly as if it was asleep; it's water clearly reflecting the moonlight.

"This seems as good as any other place," said Nat.

He lay down on a patch of damp moss. Aric took off his backpack and laid it beside him.

Nat decided to use his backpack as a pillow; Aric thought the moss would be more comfortable.

The river's soft gurgle was so soothing, a breeze rustled the millions of leaves above, it brushed against the boys' dirty skin too, it felt nice. The air smelled and tasted sweet. It was like the woods were playing a lullaby for all five senses.

There were so many stars. Aric had forgotten how many stars you could see on a camping trip.

Aric didn't care that he had no blanket, bed, or roof. The humid air kept him from being too cold, the constant breezes kept him from being too hot, the moss was so comfortable, and the stars were so bright.

It was perfect.
Aric could hear Nat softly snore.
The wood's lullaby soothed Aric's eyes shut.
Happy memories conjured up nice dreams.
Aric smiled in his sleep.

Chapter 8
Lakeside

It was very odd. Nat was dreaming, but he was awake. He hadn't opened his eyes yet and even though with the other four senses he was aware of the lake, also awake and it's rapids making a much louder sound, and the moss he was laying on, and the sun warming his skin, and the smell of sweet honey suckles, what he was seeing was his dream.

In his dream Nat saw a town, smaller than Nesserad. He saw a robbery happening on the north side, an old woman managing an inn on the south side, a bunch of kids playing in a park on the east side, the robber slipping down a hole in which a black market was happening on the west side, a happy farm on the outside of town, and in the center of the town was a beautiful silver fountain spewing sparkling blue water.

Nat had this dream every night for as long as he could remember. He knew the dream so well.

He had named the small town Lilly Town, after his mom.

Aric's voice broke into the dream, "Nat, wake up."

"Give me a second," said Nat, without opening his eyes, the end of the dream was his favorite part.

A woman was planting lilies around the beautiful fountain. The dream ended. All Nat saw was blackness.

Nat opened his eyes. Aric was standing over him with his backpack in his hand. They both could've used a bath.

"I'm starving!" said Aric.

"Me too," Nat stood up, "but our food's still with that horrible man. I have an idea; let's forage for food! There has to be some kind blueberry bush or something." Nat looked at the river, it's water was sparkling just like the fountain in his dream, "I bet if we follow this river we'll find some kind of food, and maybe even a town or something."

"Let's go then," Aric's hunger was making him cranky.

Nat brushed the dirt and moss off himself and picked up his backpack. They started walking up river going over slippery rocks, wet moss, and mud puddles; they each slipped a couple of times. Eventually the river turned into a big round lake surrounded by a ring of bright green grass.

Nat sniffed the air.

"What is it?" asked Aric.

"I think it's apples... but it might be pears," he sniffed the air again.

Aric sniffed too.

"Look!" Nat pointed.

On the other side of the lake a pear tree and an apple tree sat side by side. The boys started running, mouths already watering, but when they got there they saw that the trees were a little weird.

First off, there were bees flying back and forth between the two trees.

The fruit itself was odd too. The apple tree's fruit were all red apples on the top half and green pears on the bottom. The pear tree's fruit were green pears on top and red apple on bottom.

"Are those pears or apples?" Nat asked.

"The bees must have pollinated the trees together," said Aric.

"Are they still edible?"

"They should be."

"Well what are we waiting for?" Nat started to climb the apple-pear tree, while Aric tried jumping and grabbing the fruit from the pear-apple tree. Both attempts failed.

Neither of the trees were easy to climb and the lowest fruits were just out of reach.

"This is hopeless!" Nat plopped down on the ground in defeat.

"You know," Aric said thoughtfully, "if you let me sit on your shoulders I could reach the fruit."

"How come *you* get to sit on *my* shoulders?" asked Nat, "Why can't I sit on yours?"

"You're stronger," Aric said matter-of-factly.

"You're heavier."

"Hay! That's mean," Aric sat on the ground next to Nat.

"Well…" said Nat, "there are two trees, so you can give me a boost on one and I'll let you sit on my shoulders for the other."

Aric thought that was a good idea. So, under the apple-pear tree, they stirred up the dirt so they had a soft spot to drop the apple-pears. With some difficulty, Nat let Aric climb onto his shoulders; it was easy from there since Aric wasn't as heavy as Nat had thought. Aric dropped ten apple-pears into the patch of dirt. With a little less difficulty, Aric slid down and the boys washed the fruit in the lake.

Sitting on the lakeside with the fruit in a pile between them, the boys devoured their firsts and seconds before starting to talk.

Nat told Aric about his dream he had that morning and how it kept going even after he woke up.

"That's funny," Aric said, "That always happens to me." Aric took another bite of his third apple and said: "I wish I had normal dreams like you. Last night I dreamt I was some kind of fairy god in a mythical kingdom."

"I wish I had dreams like that," said Nat, "I've had the same dream for as long as I can remember. It gets boring sometimes."

"Well at least you don't get nightmares," Aric tossed his apple-pear core and grabbed his fourth, "one time I had a dream where I was in a black ocean and was surrounded by sharks!"

Nat thought about it. "Still sounds more exciting than the exact same dream every night," he started his fifth apple-pear.

The boys were still hungry after the apple-pears were all eaten up, so now it was Aric's turn to give Nat a boost up the pear-apple tree.

It turned out that Aric actually was pretty weak, so the boys both agreed, after all the effort to get Nat up the tree, that it would be easier and faster for Nat to lift Aric, but since Nat was already up there he went ahead and dropped about twelve pear-apples into a new patch of soft dirt they had made.

After washing them, Aric ate three before he was full and Nat ate four.

Aric packed the leftover pear-apples in his bag and the boys went over to the apple-pear tree to get some more for the road.

Just as Aric was about to climb on Nat's shoulders a silky voice called out.

"Who's there?" it said, Aric and Nat watched as a woman entered the clearing.

Chapter 9
Ms. Sandyweather

The woman was beautiful. Her pure white hair came down to her shoulders, her pale, slightly wrinkled skin brought out her light teal eyes, she was tall and skinny and her nails were painted lavender.

She wore a silk pink and purple dress with long sleeves, a long strip of the fabric stretched a few feet from her wrists, dangling as if the woman was holding two purple snakes. It looked like she wore purple, high-heeled sandals on her feet.

"Who are you?" the woman asked when she saw the boys.

It wasn't a very mean voice, firm, but not mean.

The boys just stared at her, then each other.

Finally Nat said, "I'm Nat."

"I'm Aric," Aric wasn't sure what he thought of the lady, she seemed nice…

"We got kidnapped and now we're lost," Aric suddenly blurted, "can you help us?"

The lady smiled and walked up to them. She seemed to take the kidnapping part very coolly.

"Oh yes, I can help you," she said, "My name is Ms. Sandyweather. Come, you two can tell me your story at my house."

Ms. Sandyweather turned and stepped back through the shrubbery, not even checking to see if the boys were following.

Not seeing much choice, the boys grabbed their bags and went after her.

She led them through the shrubbery to a hidden path.

"So, where is your home?" Ms. Sandyweather asked without looking back.

"Nesserad," said Nat.

"Where is that?"

"West of here," Aric said just as Nat said: "South of here." Nat and Aric looked at each other, they were definitely lost. Ms. Sandyweather didn't seem to really be listening.

The small dirt path led to another clearing, actually, it was more of a field surrounded by trees. It was covered in wildflowers of all colors; a small hill rose in the middle and on top was a pretty, white house with flower boxes in the windows.

The sun shined brightly over their heads as they followed the path up the hill and through a small, white fence that surrounded the house.

Ms. Sandyweather led them to the front door, pulled a key ring out of her pocket and fit a large, silver key into the door's lock.

Inside was a cozy little kitchen that looked like the inside of a dollhouse. There was a square table with a checkered red and pink tablecloth; a small sink was on a small counter and next to that was a wood burning stove and oven. Wooden cabinets with flower patterns were up against the flowery wallpaper. A nice, soapy smell came from a pastel blue laundry room.

Through the kitchen they went and into a den with a maroon carpet, a red and pink couch facing a red brick fireplace, a staircase that led to a second floor, and a bookshelf that took up a whole wall. It was filled with books and the occasional bookend or nick-nack.

Nat was curious about what was upstairs, but Aric was immediately drawn to the bookcase. To his disappointment, they were all cookbooks.

"Sorry it's such a mess," Ms. Sandyweather said, "I didn't plan on having guests."

The boys looked around, the place was spotless.

"Please, make yourselves at home," Ms. Sandyweather said kindly, "We'll talk about your problem in the morning. This evening you two need to rest. I'll go prepare a room for you to stay in tonight."

She went upstairs, Nat laid on the couch, and Aric went to the bookshelf, hoping to find at least one non-cookbook, but the only thing he found was a book about sewing called "Needle and Thread". Still, sewing sounded better than cooking, and learning basic sewing skills could be useful, he guessed learning how to cook is useful too, but sewing sounded at least a little more interesting.

When Aric sat at Nat's feet on the couch, about to start "Needle and Thread" Nat asked: "Why are you reading a book about sewing?"

"It couldn't hurt to learn something about sewing," Aric answered, "besides, it's the only book that's not about cooking."

Aric opened to a random page and started reading a short chapter about how to sew on buttons.

After a while Nat got bored. He tried to nap but he wasn't tired and he didn't feel like reading, especially not cookbooks. He got up and wandered through the kitchen and into the pastel colored laundry room.

Nat saw that all the clothes, the ones air-drying on a wooden rack, the ones soaking in a small tub filled with soapy, dirty water, and some lying on the floor in two small piles, were all pastel pink.

A cupboard was on one wall, painted only a slightly darker blue than the walls. Nat opened it and found two shelves of all kind of sponges and soaps and other cleaning supplies. There were also two books sitting in a small stack.

Nat picked up the first book, it was about housekeeping, no interest to him. The second book however was a book about travel entitled: "Journeys".

Nat didn't think himself too much of a traveler, but it reminded him of his dad, plus it was the only thing he could find to occupy himself.

Nat took the book to the kitchen table and flipped to the first page.

Ms. Sandyweather was upstairs for a surprisingly long time, but being absorbed in their books the boys didn't notice, which was only expected from Aric, but Nat wasn't much of a reader so it was odd that he was so absorbed.

When Ms. Sandyweather finally came down, sometime late in the evening, She asked if the boys were hungry. They knew they were as soon as she said it. Nat joined Aric on the couch.

Ms. Sandyweather ran her finger across the bookshelf from top to bottom then back to top until she suddenly snatched a cookbook off the shelf.

She started quickly flipping through the recipes while simultaneously asking the boys questions so fast that they couldn't answer.

"How many courses would you like? Do you have any allergies? Are you vegetarian or do you like meat? Do you like sweet or sour? Do you like fish? Fruit? Vegetables? Candy? Well done or medium? You know, I should just make everything."

She slammed the cookbook shut and sped into the kitchen before the boys could say anything.

The boys heard her start clanging pans and pots and then she went outside to gather firewood for the stove.

"What was that about?" asked Nat.

"She must really like cooking," Aric said.

Nat shrugged and the boys went back to their reading. Aric was reading about different needles and what to use them for. Nat was reading about Loch Ness.

Ms. Sandyweather came back with the wood. Had they not been so intrigued in reading they would have offered to help.

After a while Aric came to the end of a chapter that gave tips on how to make clothes. He took a minute to look out the window.

Aric could see the sky growing from pink to purple as the big orange ball sank below the horizon.

He sat his book on the sofa. *Wasn't noon only a few minutes ago?* He wondered. He must have been reading for a long time.

Time was so ironic. Good days pass too quickly, and bad days are too long.

In the back of his head Aric recalled someone saying that time was like a rubber band, there is only so much of it but you can stretch it out and make it seem like more.

Aric had learned a lot in the past hours. He'd never sewn before but he felt confident he was a natural at it, and he rarely felt confident. He already had ideas for clothes to make. Taking up sewing probably wasn't going to help his lack of friends, but he was willing to try it anyway.

Just as the sun was out of sight, Ms. Sandyweather came in announcing that dinner was ready.

Ms. Sandyweather had made them an excellent five-course dinner, each course tasting better than the last.

After dinner Ms. Sandyweather told the boys that they should go to sleep and that they would talk about the kidnapping thing in the morning. She led the boys up the stairs and to the back of the first of two maroon hallways, to a light yellow door.

"This is the room I have prepared for you," said Ms. Sandyweather.

She opened the door and led the boys in.

The walls and floor of the room matched the light yellow door, an occasional pink and blue flower pattern was on the wall, there was one window with pink and blue striped curtains.

In the center of the room was a small, wooden card table with two chairs and a chess set with pink and blue pieces and squares. Two twin beds sat each with a light green and lavender patterned quilt, one bed had a light green pillow and the other had a lavender one.

"Goodnight," Ms. Sandyweather said, she closed the odd colored door and left the boys in the odd colored room.

"I'm not very tired," said Aric.

"Me neither."

"Want to play a game of chess?"

Nat shrugged, "Sure."

By the time they were halfway through the game they were both tired. They started getting ready for bed without resetting the chess set.

Nat kicked off his sandals and lay on top of the covers, he immediately fell asleep.

Aric went over to the window. He liked the way the moonlight reflected off the tops of the trees. It looked like an enchanted forest.

He stood there awhile looking at the view and listening to Nat's soft snores. He had come over to shut the curtains but he left them open.

He decided to reset the chessboard.

Wishing for a bath and warm pajamas Aric took off his shoes and got under the covers, sitting up with his back against the yellow headboard.

Aric stared out the window at the moonlit woods, he could hear crickets chirping.

Then he heard another noise, not Nat's snoring or crickets, but a rustling sound coming from the other side of the wall. That must be Ms. Sandyweather's bedroom, she must still be awake.

Aric usually found night noises soothing, like his parents talking downstairs or distant thunder or crickets or an owl hooting, but for some reason Aric didn't find anything soothing about the sounds coming from the other side of the wall...

Chapter 10
Under the Bed

About two hours had gone by and Aric still hadn't fallen asleep. The noises coming from Ms. Sandyweather's bedroom bothered him, he didn't know why.

Aric sat up and looked at the window, it was closer to midnight and the moon was almost overhead and the distant woods seemed brighter.

For the first time Aric recognized the sounds he was hearing as talking. *Is Ms. Sandyweather talking to herself?* Wondered Aric.

Aric wondered if he should wake Nat, Ms. Sandyweather being up so long was starting to creep him out, and now she was talking to herself? Or someone? Then again, if it were nothing Nat would be pretty mad.

By now Aric's overactive imagination was casting shadows on the forest outside. He better wake Nat.

As quietly as he could, Aric went over and nudged Nat's shoulder.

"Nat?" he whispered.

Nat gave a small grunt.

Aric nudged Nat's shoulder harder.

"Nat!" he whispered again.

"What?" Nat groaned, keeping his eyes shut.

"Shh!" whispered Aric, "I think Ms. Sandyweather is up to something. She's talking to someone in her room, I heard her through the wall."

"Then why don't you check it out?" Nat rolled over in his bed and went back to sleep.

Nat was going to be no help. Aric would have to figure out what Ms. Sandyweather was doing himself. Rats!

Aric tiptoed into the dark, maroon hallway. He tried to be brave as he reluctantly crept down the hall.

The courage he had was very quickly used up.

Aric remembered his mother saying that whenever she was scared she pretended to be someone or something she thought was brave.

Nat seemed pretty fearless to Aric. Aric continued down the hall, picturing himself as Nat.

When he reached the stairs the hall turned to the right. There were no portraits of people, just flowers and cool looking bottles that were arranged neatly and reminded Aric of wizard's lairs.

There were no doors in the hall except at the very end; the one on the right must be Ms. Sandyweather's room. Another door was across from it.

An eerie green light leaked through the cracks and keyhole of Ms. Sandyweather's bedroom door.

That would of made Aric run back to the room and hide under the pastel covers, but since he was Nat right now it wasn't as scary. It was a good thing that Aric had such a good imagination.

As he got closer Aric could hear Ms. Sandyweather pacing. He was going so quietly and slowly that he wasn't sure he was moving at all, he couldn't even tell if he was holding his breath or not.

He must of been moving because eventually he found himself squatting on the maroon carpet, which was an ugly brownish color in the eerie green light, and putting his eye to the keyhole.

All he could see was Ms. Sandyweather's back and her bed. The emerald light seemed to come from underneath the bed and every now and then he thought he saw movement there.

By now Aric was close enough to make out Ms. Sandyweather's annoyed whispers.

"You have to wait until midnight," she said, "then you can eat them."

Aric lost his balance and fell on the floor.

"What was that?" said another voice that was deeper and kind of creepy.

What would Nat do now? Aric wondered, *He would definitely think fast, but…*

Aric just remembered the other door. He got up and quickly opened the other door, it was a coat closet. He got in and shut the door just before he heard Ms. Sandyweather open her door. He prayed that she wouldn't check the closet.

Ms. Sandyweather went down the hall a few steps, then, being convinced that it was just the old, creaky house, she went back to her room and closed the door.

Aric mustered up Nat's courage and quietly returned to his place at the keyhole.

"You can't come out until midnight," said Ms. Sandyweather, "you know that, it's a rule." Her voice was getting more annoyed.

"But I'm starving!" said the voice in a little more than a whisper.

"Shh!" hushed Ms. Sandyweather, "Well that's too bad then! It's still half an hour till midnight so your hunger will have to wait. You know very well that five minutes after you'll have a full stomach. They're not going anywhere! They're sleeping in the next room."

Aric had heard as much as he could take. He knew he and Nat should get out fast!

As quickly as he could without alerting Ms. Sandyweather, Aric went back to the guest room.

"Nat!" Aric whispered, "Nat! Wake up!"

"What?" Nat growled.

"Ms. Sandyweather's going to feed us to some monster or something!"

"Don't be ridiculous," said Nat, "Ms. Sandyweather's not-"

"Come listen! You can hear her talking to something in her room!"

Nat sighed and got out of bed.

"Fine," he said, "but I think you're just hearing things."

Aric led Nat to the wall and he put his ear up to it, he could hear two whispering voices.

"You're right, there are two voices in there. She's definitely up to something. We better get out of here. Grab your bag."

"Wait," said Aric, "let's make our beds first."

Nat looked at Aric like he was a crazy person, "Are you kidding!?" he said.

"It doesn't feel right to leave them unmade."

"Aric, we have to get out of here as fast as we can!"

"It'll only take a second, and you don't have to make yours."

Nat knew that this argument was wasting time so he let Aric make his bed.

While Aric was making his bed, Nat decided to make his own. He hadn't gotten in the covers so it just needed straightening out, besides, there was nothing else to do.

Nat rolled his eyes as Aric fluffed his pillow, then he picked up the books that Ms. Sandyweather had let them bring up from the floor.

"Should we take these?" Nat asked Aric, he was secretly hoping to keep "Journeys."

"No, that's stealing," Aric took "Needle and Thread" and placed it on his perfectly made bed. Nat dropped his book on his half-heartedly made bed, he didn't like to leave behind his book, which was odd since Aric was the book person and he seemed fine leaving his book behind.

Nat grabbed his backpack, "You ready now?"

"Uh, yeah, just let me do something first, I'll meet you in the kitchen."

"Ok," Nat sighed, he started sneaking downstairs.

As soon as Nat was out of sight, Aric fished all his pencils out of his backpack, placed them on his bed, stuffed "Journeys" into his backpack and went out the door. He knew it was technically stealing, but leaving behind the pencils made him feel just a little better.

Nat was waiting in the kitchen.

"You ready?" he asked.

"Yes," Aric said.

"I think that Ms. Sandyweather's bedroom window is right over the door so we're going to have to keep our backs to the wall then run for the woods."

"Ok."

Nat quietly opened the door. The field was flooded with the eerie light from Ms. Sandyweather's window. He shivered.

"Ok, come on," said Nat, "I'll tell you when we need to start running."

Nat went out the door, Aric followed. They kept their backpacks to the side of the house and edged to the left. Both boys stared up at Ms. Sandyweather's window.

"Now!" said Nat.

The boys darted over the gate and ran until they reached the edge of the clearing, they looked back. The silhouette of a woman appeared in the window.

They ducked into the shrubbery and ran as fast as they could. After a minute or two, Nat tripped on an out-sticking root. Aric stopped and helped Nat up.

"Are you ok?" asked Aric.

"Yah, I'm fine," said Nat, rubbing his scraped knee, "but I think we should take a break."

Nat was panting and sweating. Aric, who was better at pacing himself, wasn't doing so much panting and sweating.

Nat dropped his backpack on the ground and sat with his back against a tree. Aric took his backpack off too and sat with Nat.

After he had caught his breath, Aric randomly said, "I'm glad we made our beds."

"Why?" Nat asked through gasping, he still hadn't got his breath.

"Well, what if Ms. Sandyweather wasn't really up to something?" said Aric, "She would think we were kidnapped again or something."

After Nat had caught his breath, he said, "Now I wish we had left a note. You have pencils and some paper don't you?"

"Well paper," said Aric, "I left all my pencils at Ms. Sandyweather's."

"What?!" asked Nat.

"I left them in trade for this." Aric pulled "Journeys" from his backpack and handed it to Nat.

"I thought that taking the books was stealing," said Nat.

"Well not if you leave something in return," argued Aric.

"But it's not like it was up for trade or anything."

"True..."

"Also, why didn't you take your sewing book?"

"Well, I like a lot of books, but this is the first book I've seen you read without taking a break every five minutes."

Nat chuckled.

"I still not convinced that it's okay to take things, even if you leave something behind, but thanks anyway," he said.

"Well, you're the one who suggested stealing them in the first place," Aric pointed out.

"I guess so," said Nat, "Well we can't return it now, if Ms. Sandyweather's really wanting to feed us to some under-the-bed monster or in-the-closet monster or whatever it was, then she's probably already discovered that we're gone."

"What do you think will happen when she finds our beds empty?" asked Aric.

"She'll probably be angry, or upset, or confused, maybe worried? I dunno, she may come looking for us," said Nat.

The boys were silent for a moment. Some crickets started their song.

"Are you tired?" Aric asked.

"Yes, but I don't think I'll be able to sleep."

"Me neither," said Aric, "should we keep going?"

"I think that would be a good idea," said Nat, he dropped "Journeys" into his backpack and the boys started walking through the dark woods.

Chapter 11
For the Compass

"I can't take another step," said Aric, exhausted.

"Me neither," said Nat, who was equally exhausted, but coping better.

Both boys sat down in the mixture of ankle high grass and moss. Aric lay down and almost immediately fell asleep, Nat did the same, they were too tired to be scared anymore.

Soon the sunlight was putting a gold tent on the tops of the trees and making its way down to the boys. When it got to them through the millions of leaves it covered them like a warm, golden blanket, and small gusts of wind blew their hair around.

The boys slept as the beautiful morning turned into a beautiful afternoon, and as the beautiful afternoon turned into a nice, cool evening clouds covered the sky spreading a gray-blue tent on the world, and the sound of crickets replaced the birds' chirping.

Aric's eyes opened. He wondered where he was, and then remembered.

He sat up. Nat was still sleeping beside him. He looked around. The grey-blue tent was kind of magical looking. The quick, dim light of a firefly appeared a few yards away.

Aric felt very rested now. He gently nudged Nat awake.

"It's morning," said Aric, "uh, I mean, it's afternoon… I think."

Nat looked around, "We better start going again," he said in a not-quite-fully-awake voice.

Nat got up slowly, picked up his backpack, and started walking sluggishly away.

Aric got up, scooped up his own backpack and hurried after Nat. A frog croaked in the distance. Aric wondered if there was a creek somewhere nearby. His stomach growled.

"Can we stop and eat breakfast or dinner or lunch or something?" he asked.

"Let's walk a little longer, then we will," Nat answered, he was hungry too, and still not fully awake, but he wanted to go a little longer since they were already going.

Eventually, Nat said they could stop, his own hunger, plus Aric's whining and begging, drove him to it.

The boys stopped at a little ring of rocks with a small tree growing in the middle. They each sat on a flat rock, they weren't very comfortable but they were something to sit on. The boys started searching in their packs for food.

Nat didn't find any food, but Aric still had five pair-apples left from the lakeside.

The boys had two each, Nat took the last one and put it in the bag the apples had been in. Aric put the bag in his backpack and they started walking again.

The evening was darkening surprisingly slow; it was like the day didn't want to end.

The noise of rustling leaves came from behind the boys.

"Did you hear that?" Aric stopped.

"Hear what?" asked Nat.

The rustling sound came again and this time Nat heard it too. Then suddenly, out of the shrubs the hermit dashed out with a cry of anger.

Both boys screamed and ran as fast as they could with the hermit quickly catching up.

"Nat!" yelled Aric, "I think he want's the compass!"

Nat would have dropped the compass if the hermit weren't sure to catch him if he stopped to dig in his backpack.

Then the boys heard a thud and looked back to see that the hermit had caught his leg in a tree root and was struggling to get out.

Nat whipped off his backpack and frantically searched through it. As he pulled the compass out the root snapped and the hermit started after them again.

Nat dropped the compass on the ground and he and Aric sprinted away as fast as they could go.

After a while Aric realized that the hermit wasn't chasing them anymore. He stopped and called to Nat to stop.

"He's... gone," Aric said between pants.

After they had finally caught their breath Nat said, "I guess we should keep walking then."

Aric nodded in agreement. "But I think we should rest a while first" he said.

The sun, even though it had gone under the horizon by now, had let it's light stay and keep the sky dimly lit.

After taking a short rest the boys started off again. The woods had slowly gotten a lot thicker.

They pushed branches and vines out of their way, they crunched hundreds of sticks under their feet with every step, and they couldn't see a yard ahead of themselves.

"When did it get so thick?" Aric complained behind Nat, his legs were getting itchy.

"Ouch!" Nat yelled, a sharp stick had poked his arm, "I don't know, but I hope it clears up soon."

The boys pushed through the shrubbery and found themselves on a dirt road.

"Wow," said Aric, "this road is big enough for a carriage!"

"Exactly," said Nat, "look, wheel tracks, this must lead somewhere, like a town! We could get help there!"

"I just hope it doesn't lead to another hermit's house."

"I don't think it will. It most likely leads to a town or a city maybe."

"Well, which way should we go?" asked Aric.

Nat looked in one direction, then the other.

"Left," he said pointing.

As he and Aric started down the dirt road, Aric hoped they wouldn't run into anything as bad or worse than a crazy hermit or weird lady.

They had no idea where or to what the road would take them, and they wouldn't find out until they got there.

Chapter 12
The Garden by the Sea

It didn't take long for the road to lead the boys to a seaside town.

The boys exited the woods, in front of them was a slope going down to a town full of houses, small gardens, and shops. It was a nice, friendly looking town.

Past the town there were docks stretching out into the ocean and tied to them were some small sailboats with fishermen unloading today's catch into barrels. A few boats were still out in the sea, but would probably be docking soon.

Aric smiled, he loved the sea.

Nat was gaping at the huge body of water. He had never seen the ocean, he had heard it was big, but he didn't think it was this big! It went so far he couldn't see the end of it. Did it even end somewhere? All he could see was the fine line between the navy blue water and the graying sky.

On a hill, to the right of the town, was a big mansion with a dirt path leading from the town to it's front door.

"Do you think we should go to the town or to there?" Aric asked pointing to the town and then the mansion.

Nat was still in awe of the sea when he said, "I dunno." He wasn't really listening to Aric.

"I think we should go to that big house," said Aric.

Nat shook himself out of his trance, "Let's go and see if that wall is a walled garden." he pointed to the wall sticking out from the mansion.

"Why?" asked Aric.

"If it is we could spend the night there," being in the woods for so long and being two kids alone made Nat feel like they should keep hidden.

"Ok," said Aric, he liked the idea of sleeping in a garden.

Nat took one more look at the big blue sea. It was like a ground sky. He watched a white line of foam on top of a wave make its way to the docks and disappear. He followed Aric.

The mansion looked like it was made of smooth stone, and even though most of it's many windows were dark, it was very inviting. Nat thought there must be a big fireplace in there with a nice, comfy, red velvet chair to nap in, and warm bedrooms with big soft beds with canopies, and a big long banquet table with a feast for one hundred people.

When the boys reached the wall they immediately found an arched entrance.

A magical blue tent from the last light of day covered everything in the big garden.

The stonewalls were covered in ivy, a small oak tree grew in a corner, and flowers of all shapes, sizes, and colors were growing everywhere, on trees, bushes, or from the ground. There were hundreds of fireflies everywhere.

Aric went over to a bush he thought was covered in multicolored flowers but it turned out to be sleeping butterflies, there was even a cocoon.

An arch in a big hedge led to a second section of the garden.

In the center of the second part was a marble fountain that looked an aqua color, silvery water trickled from it's top to the small pool at the bottom. A paved path went around the fountain and went up to the door where you enter the house. There were more flowers and fireflies and ivy on the walls.

Everything in the garden was gentle and soft. The fountain's trickling, the blue-grey darkening light, the fading in and out of the bugs' yellow and green lights, the distant sound of the ocean.

"Let's sleep here," said Nat.

"But I'm not tired," said Aric, "we've only been awake for about an hour."

"I know, but we need to get back in the habit of sleeping at night and doing stuff in the day."

Aric wasn't sleepy, but the garden made him feel like sleeping anyway.

The fountain reminded Nat of his dream. He went straight to the fountain and lay on the edge of it. It took him awhile since he wasn't very tired either, but he managed to fall asleep.

Nat saw his dream, but one thing was different, he saw the gardener's face.

It was Lilly.

Chapter 13
Mr. Angel

The door to the garden opened and out came a man. The man had kind, brown eyes, dark, graying hair, and a kind handsome face. He wore a light brown tweed jacket and matching trousers.

On this nice, breezy day the man had decided to go out to the garden to get some herbs for his breakfast, some roses to brighten up the dining room, and some fresh air to start off the day.

When the man saw the two boys sleeping on his fountain he was not as surprised as you may think. He had seen a lot of odd things in his long life and this wasn't in the top fifty.

Instead of waking the boys or getting mad for them trespassing, he quietly cut some herbs and a bouquet of pink roses and went back inside.

He put the roses in a nice vase and left the herbs in the kitchen for later. He grabbed the book he had been reading from his private library and went back out to the garden.

When he came back outside he saw that the wind was blowing in clouds. It was going to be a rainy afternoon.

The last thing Aric remembered was looking for a place to sleep, he had followed Nat's lead to the fountain.

Aric sat up groggily, it was a nice and breezy late morning, Aric could tell by the sun position. He saw the man sitting between him and Nat. He stared, stunned.

The man looked up from his book. "Good morning," he said naturally, as if they slept in his garden all the time.

Aric looked for his voice, he couldn't find it.

"I hope you had a good sleep," the man continued, when Aric still didn't speak he said, "You're all dirty, like you've been on a long trip."

Aric stole a quick glance at his reflection in the water, his clothes were covered in dirt stains, there was a small tear in his pants knee and his hair was like there was a hedgehog on his head. Nat was about the same but had a hole in each pant leg.

"Are you mute?" the man asked, not like it was a question, but in a way that says, "Will you speak already?" He put down his book.

"Uh... no, sir," Aric's voice finally came out of hiding.

"I'm glad," said the man, "I hope you and your friend are well."

"Um, yes, sir,"

"Now, I feel I should ask what you two are doing in my garden," The man said.

Aric winced, "I, uh... well... I think Nat could tell it better," he blurted.

"Is that his name? Nat?" The man said, gesturing to the sleeping figure next to him.

"Uh, yes, sir," Aric wondered if telling this stranger Nat's name was a good idea.

"And your name is?" the man asked politely.

"Aric," He still wasn't sure about telling this stranger his name, but he wasn't going to lie!

"My name is Angel Wilson," said the man, "most everybody here calls me Mr. Angel."

Mr. Angel held out his hand and Aric reluctantly shook it.

Mr. Angel then turned and nudged Nat awake, "Good morning Nat," he said.

Nat looked surprised and confused.

"Aric already told me your name," explained Mr. Angel, "you can call me Mr. Angel."

Nat shook Mr. Angel's hand too.

"Now, Aric told me you could explain why you spent the night with my roses," Mr. Angel said.

"Well, you see Mr. Angel, me and Aric got kidnapped by some guys in black robes and we both escaped from them, but we got lost in the woods and when we found our way out we needed a place to sleep and we thought this garden might be a nice place."

"Those woods over toward the east?" Mr. Angel asked.

"Yes sir, I think so," Nat said.

"No need for 'sir'," Mr. Angel said, "Can you describe what the kidnappers looked like?"

"Well," said Nat, "it was really dark so it's hard to tell, but they were wearing all black. They had capes with hoods and big boots."

"There were a lot of them," Aric jumped in, "and they had a horse and wagon."

"Oh, yes," said Mr. Angel, "I've heard of them."

"You have?!" asked Aric.

"Who are they?" Nat asked.

"The Black-Hoods," Mr. Angel said.

"What are they?" asked Nat, "I know they're kidnappers, but are they like some kind of pirates?"

"Are you hungry?" Mr. Angel asked suddenly.

"Yes!" said Aric.

"What are the Black-Hoods?!" Nat was getting frustrated.

"I'll tell you who and what they are after brunch." Mr. Angel got up and headed for the door to his house, he beckoned for the boys to follow, leaving Nat feeling very annoyed.

The dining room was shaped like a big octagon. Four of it's walls held big windows looking out to the ocean, while the other four each held a big portrait.

Mr. Angel had placed Nat and Aric at the round dining room table with a vase of Mr. Angel's fresh pink roses for a centerpiece. Mr. Angel was in the kitchen preparing brunch.

Aric stared out the window at the sea. He could see the sails of fishermen's ships as they searched for a good fishing spot to bring in a profit.

"Do you live by yourself Mr. Angel?" Aric called into the kitchen.

"Yes," Mr. Angel called back.

"Don't you at least have servants?" Aric asked.

"I don't need servants."

"None at all?"

"What kind of servants are you talking about?"

"A maid?"

"This place never gets that messy, and if it did I could clean it myself."

"A butler?"

"What would I use a butler for?"

"To do things for you."

"Whatever needs to be done I can do myself."

"What about a nanny?"

Mr. Angel walked into the room with a basket of breakfast pastries, "You're very talkative, aren't you Aric?" Mr. Angel said, "No, all my children are grown up and have nannies for their own children. And before you ask, I definitely don't need a cook."

Mr. Angel passed the pastries to Aric. Aric took one and handed the basket to Nat. Mr. Angel went back into the kitchen to finish his cooking.

Nat took one of the homemade crescent-moon shaped pastries and took a bite; it was delicious, light, and fluffy. If you could make bread from nothing but icing, it would taste like that pastry.

Nat, being a little overwhelmed at the ocean view sat with his back to it. Instead, he looked at the portraits on the opposite walls.

The first was an elderly woman sitting in a big, pink chair. The second one looked like a younger Mr. Angel and his wife at their wedding. The third was a family portrait of Mr. Angel, his wife, and four kids. The fourth looked like the four kids all grown.

A little later Mr. Angel brought in a tray with three scrambled eggs, made with herbs from the garden, and buttered toast. Mr. Angel asked what drink the boys would like, Aric got milk and Nat got apple juice. Mr. Angel put cranberry jam on his toast, he offered it to the boys, but neither of them liked cranberries.

Nat took a bite of toast, "Who are the Black-Hoods?" he demanded.

"Yes, now for that story," Mr. Angel said, he put his elbows on the table, held his hands together, and rested his head on his knuckles, "You probably already know that they're kidnappers that have been in the business for a long time, and even though they're not too smart, they've never been caught. Aric, would you like more milk?"

"No, thank you," Aric wiped away a milk-stash.

"Keep going," Nat took another bite of his eggs.

"Well," said Mr. Angel, "before I retired, I worked as a detective, the police and I searched for the Black-Hoods for years, all we figured out is that they travel through secret paths in the woods and then the trail ends at Bork. We figured they must put their hostages on boats and smuggle them to other countries to sell as slaves." Mr. Angel took a sip of his tea.

"Well if you know they're at Bork how come you didn't just catch them there?" Nat asked.

"Well,-" started Mr. Angel.

"Wait, does this mean our friends are going to be sold as slaves?!" Aric said shrilly.

"It was only a theory, Aric," said Mr. Angel.

"But that still means that they might be!" said Nat, "Hey, why don't we go to Bork and catch them!"

"It's not as easy as that," argued Mr. Angel, "Bork is a huge city, and I bet the Black-Hoods have secret hideouts to stay in until their boat meets them."

"But it's worth a shot isn't it?" asked Nat.

Mr. Angel considered it. "Where did you get kidnapped from?"

"Nesserad," said Nat.

"And they were in a carriage?"

"They had a wagon," said Aric.

"Let's see," Mr. Angel looked up, "from Nesserad to Bork by wagon through the woods.

How long would that be? How long has it been since you got kidnapped?" he asked the boys.

"Years!" exclaimed Aric.

"It's been about a week," said Nat.

"Well, from Nesserad to Bork would take maybe a little more than a week," said Mr. Angel.

"So we have a chance at catching them?!" Nat was getting excited.

"Maybe," said Mr. Angel, "If we were to go, the fastest way is by boat, which I could arrange easily."

"Well we have to go then!" Nat hopped out of his chair, knocking it to the floor.

"What do you think Aric?" asked Mr. Angel.

"Well…" Aric grabbed another pastry, "I guess we can't just let them be sold, I don't see how we couldn't go and at least try."

Mr. Angel nodded; Aric could tell he was thinking the same thing.

"I'll go down to the docks after breakfast and hire a ship to take us."

Nat could tell by the way that Mr. Angel practically gobbled down his eggs and toast that he missed his old detective work and was excited to momentarily come out of retirement. When he was done, Mr. Angel took his dishes to the kitchen. As he came back he said: "I'm going down to the docks. When you finish your meals, just put your dirty dishes in the dish tub. You two stay here, I'll be back in about an hour." Then he hurried away.

The boys finished their meals, put their dishes in the washtub in the kitchen, sat on the floor next to the big windows and looked out.

Aric wondered how deep the ocean might be, and Nat wondered why they had so quickly come to trust Mr. Angel, quickly trusting in people hadn't exactly been much help to them so far.

"Let's explore," said Nat.

"But, Mr. Angel told us to stay in the house," said Aric.

"I just meant around the house, it's not like we're going to hurt anything."

Nat stood up and walked into an entry hall, Aric reluctantly followed.

"Cool," Nat gasped.

Aric stared.

The hall was huge. It was flooded with natural light from big windows, big, wooden double doors were on one side, and on the other side, the red carpet ran up the big staircase to a balcony on the second floor, which, in a normal sized house, would be about four stories high. A bright chandelier hung from the high roof. Beautiful oil paintings lined the walls.

"Wow," said Aric.

Nat started for the stairs.

"Hey, wait," said Aric, "I want to look at the paintings."

Nat sighed, "Fine," he said.

Surprisingly, after a while, Nat got very engrossed looking at the paintings.

There were eight paintings. The first was a picture of tall, white trees with black splotches, it had a golden, red-orange background was a tell-tale sign of autumn.

The second was a picture of someone's office with a desk pushed against the navy blue wall.

The third was the beach at sunset.

The fourth was a herd of wild mustangs running through a yellowy-green field.

The fifth was of a tall, purple mountain that reached the clouds.

The sixth looked like a bunch of grown-ups at a party. They were all sipping red wine from fancy cups, dancing, or talking.

The seventh was a tired looking man working at a desk.

The last looked like a portrait of Mr. Angel when he was Nat and Aric's age.

Nat wondered how the artists had gotten so good, he also wondered if he could ever learn to be that good, he decided that he would try drawing something sometime.

After they looked at the paintings for a while, Mr. Angel came through the double doors.

"Ok," said Mr. Angel, "I've hired a friend of mine to take us to Bork on his ship, we leave first thing in the morning."

"Yay!" said Aric, he loved being on ships.

Nat was excited too, but also a little nervous about being on a ship on the big sea, even if they weren't going too far from shore.

Chapter 14
Sleeping World

Nat watched the big orange ball that was the sun slowly creep it's way below the horizon.

The boys sat in the guest room that Mr. Angel had led them to after dinner. It was big and octagon shaped like the dinning room was, except it was painted a cooling blue.

Aric laid on the queen sized bed he and Nat had agreed to share, despite Mr. Angel's offer to pull up a cot.

Nat had pulled a chair up to the big window and rested his head and arms on the windowsill.

The window had long green curtains that matched the ones on the bed. It had an extraordinary view, Nat could see the town, the woods he and Aric had been lost in only the day before, and the magnificent sunset reflecting off the water of the sea.

To Nat, the town seemed like a person getting ready for bed. The number of lights in windows was slowly decreasing, as well as the number of people on the road.

Nat wondered about the ocean. It seemed like something magical. It was like the bed curtains, it hid everything on it's other side. Beauty. Danger. He guessed the woods were the same way, and so were the walls and roofs of the houses. That excited him, scared him, and filled him with wonder.

The sea was big and blue, like a second sky on the ground.

The forest, like the ocean, was big and went as far as the eye could see.

The ocean was a sea of water. The woods were a sea of trees.

The ocean was a second sky. The woods were a second sea.

The water was a sea of blue. The woods were a sea of green.

The water. The trees. The air. The people. They were all seas, just in different ways.

"Aric?" Nat asked.

"Yes?" answered Aric.

"Do you still have some paper left over?"

"I think so," Aric put down the book Mr. Angel had loaned him and picked his backpack up from the floor. After digging a while Aric pulled out a few pieces of slightly crumpled paper and brought it over to Nat.

"I don't have anymore pencils though," Aric told Nat as he handed him the yellowing paper.

"I've got one," Nat said.

Aric went back to his reading as Nat produced his own pencil from his backpack.

The windowsill was big enough to lay the paper out on. Nat took the pencil and tried to draw the view from the window. He got the flower boxes in the windows of the small town, the long shadows the forest was casting into itself, the darkening shades of color in the sky, which was difficult with no colored pencils, and the sun sinking behind the sea as if it was pulling it over it's head and planned on using it like a blanket to sleep under.

Nat finished and looked at his work, he didn't think much of it. In truth it was pretty good for a ten-year-old boy who'd never even drawn many doodles in his schoolbooks.

Even though Nat thought his work was kind of bad, he decided he would try again, but not now. Now, he was tired.

Nat neatly folded the drawing and set it in his backpack. Aric felt too tired to continue reading.

Nat left the curtains drawn at the window, as Aric shut the ones at the bed. Nat crawled into the bed, as Aric reached to turn out the reading light.

"Goodnight, Nat."

"Night, Aric."

Nat got under the covers, his head at the foot of the bed in order to see the window better, he pulled the bed curtains open just a crack so he could see.

In the darkness of the room, Nat watched the sky go from pink, to orange, to red, to purple. Watched the stars start shining one by one, shyly at first, then bolder and brighter. Watched sky become a blue so dark you could call it black.

He watched the shadows grow longer in the woods.

He watched the line that separates sky and sea vanish.

He watched as one by one, the houses go dark.

He watched the sea of water,

the sea of air,

the sea of people,

the sea of color,

and the sea of trees fall asleep.

And he did the same.

Chapter 15
Gifts on the Second Sky

The huge dock was covered in people scattering about to and fro trying to get off or on their ships for a holiday or business or whatever else they had in mind.

Nat and Aric stood off to the side as Mr. Angel talked to the captain of the ship they would soon be boarding.

Aric felt excited. His dad had loved ships and boats so sailing was a normal thing for him. He loved how weird it felt at first to be on something rocking back and forth, and it was even better after you got used to it.

Aric's dad had been saving up to buy their own boat before the flood.

Nat was kind of nervous though. Three days ago, seeing the ocean in person hadn't been something he'd ever done, let alone had sailed it on a monstrous ship.

Nat looked at the ship they were going to ride on. It was very big, had a ramp so you could get onto it, and was stained brownish with greenish trim. It wasn't actually meant for passengers, it had a few rooms for the crew, which the boys and Mr. Angel would stay in, but it was mainly a cargo ship, the only reason Mr. Angel could get them a ride in it was because he was such good friends with the captain. The big sails rolled in the wind as the crew loaded big crates onto the ship. How did something so big float on the water?

The captain started up the ramp, and Mr. Angel walked over to the boys.

"The captain says the ship will leave in about half an hour," said Mr. Angel, "Let's get onboard."

Seeing the land from the water was weird and cool at the same time.

A gust of salty wind blew through Nat's hair, it felt good, despite the bit of seasickness he had, everything around him smelled like salt water.

Aric had his back propped against one of the big cargo crates, he was writing on his scrap paper with a pen the captain had kindly given him since Ms. Sandyweather had all his pencils.

Nat leaned against the railing, watching the land slowly fade away like a ghost in the early morning mist. Suddenly, Nat had an urge to try and draw it.

"Hey, Aric, do you still have any extra paper?"

"Yah, it's in my backpack. You can get it."

Aric went back to his writing while Nat sat next to him and rummaged through Aric's backpack, and was surprised at what he found.

Nat pulled the dagger from Aric's backpack and stared at it. It had a strawberry red handle and a lightning bolt shaped blade.

Aric looked up and saw Nat staring at his dad's dagger.

"You can have that if you want," said Aric, "I don't want it."

The words had come out before Aric had thought about it, and he was glad they did.

Nat was surprised and happy when Aric offered him the knife. But he felt a little guilty. It was such a great knife and had an almost perfectly sharp blade. Aric's dad had only ever used it as a letter opener every now and then.

He felt like he needed to give Aric something in return. He got an idea.

Nat grabbed his own backpack and fished for his journal he never used. He held it out to Aric.

"Here, you can have this."

Aric's eyes lit up, he took the journal and stared down at it's leather cover in his lap.

"Thank you," Aric said.

Nat sat beside Aric and both boys stared at their gifts.

The loud ship horn blared. Nat couldn't see the land anymore, but he didn't care. Instead, he took the paper from Aric's pack and his pencil and started drawing the knife; he thought it would be a good way to examine every detail of it. After awhile he decided to draw it laying on an open journal.

As soon as Aric had taken in the fact that he had a journal again, he immediately opened it and started the first page. He wrote:

I have this journal because Nat gave it to me. I think he's really nicer than he thinks he is.

Aric looked down at his handwriting, he loved to see it between the lined pages.

My dad's knife was like the thing I store all my bad memories and thoughts in, and now that Nat has it it's like all I've ever had is good times and good thoughts. Like a very clean slate. No, not a clean slate, a brand new one!

Aric thought about what to write next. He decided to write about the adventure he and Nat had been on:

This is how Nat and I became friends...

Chapter 16
Bork in the Early Morning

"We're here," Mr. Angel's voice came from the door.

Nat opened his eyes, he and Aric were in bed in the cabin the captain had let them and Mr. Angel spend the night in. The brown beds weren't the most comfortable place to sleep and the matching blankets were a little scratchy, but they were still better than moss and dirt.

When the boys didn't get up Mr. Angel said, "The ship just docked at Bork, we need to get off board in less than an hour."

Nat turned and looked out the round porthole. It was still dark out. The line that separates sky and sea was still invisible. You could only tell them apart by looking at the heap of twinkling stars.

Mr. Angel went over to Aric, still asleep, and shook him gently awake.

Aric sat up, "Are we there?" he asked sleepily.

"Yes," Mr. Angel said.

Aric sprang out of bed.

Nat rolled onto his stomach, "What time is it?" he asked.

"Five twenty," Mr. Angel sat his own bag on Aric's bed and pulled out two pairs of khaki pants and two boldly colored button up shirts, one green one blue. He laid them on Aric's bed and pointed to the little bathroom.

"The captain left you soap, and I left a comb in there," he said, "both of you need to get a good, quick shower, comb those rat's nests out of your hair, and put on these clothes I bought you. Now be quick about it. I want us to be off the ship in thirty minutes or less. Meet me on the dock when you're done and make sure you don't leave anything behind. Got that Nat?"

Nat grunted a "yes," from under his pillow.

Mr. Angel left the room, shutting the door behind him.

Aric looked at the clothes Mr. Angel had left, "Do you want the blue shirt or the green one?" he asked.

"I don't care," Nat still had his head under the pillow.

Aric shrugged and grabbed the green shirt and a pair of khakis and went into the bathroom.

Nat fell asleep.

Clean, fresh, and in their new clothes, Nat and Aric went up to the deck. It was still dark, stars still twinkled like lanterns hung high in the sky, but were fading quickly, and a thin line of gold sat on the horizon.

Nat was still a little groggy; it took Aric awhile to make him get out of bed.

The boys found Mr. Angel watching the crew unload.

"Ready?" Mr. Angel asked.

"Ready." the boys answered.

Nat looked out at Bork. It was a pretty town, even at night. Streetlights cast orange circles on the road where every now and then there would be a person walking by or a horse drawn cab. In the distance, you could tell the town was much busier near the center of the city.

The distant sound of a clock tower bell announced six o'clock.

"You two look nice in those clothes," Mr. Angel said as he led them towards the ramp, "Where are your old ones?"

"In our bags," Nat gestured to the backpack on his back.

"Good, we'll drop them off at a cleaner's," Mr. Angel said, "The captain said he arranged for a cab to pick us up, it should be here anytime now."

The boys and Mr. Angel thanked and said goodbye to the captain and went off the ship to the road and waited for their cab.

A few minutes later an open cab stopped in front of them. It was painted black with two matching black horses pulling it, it was on big, round, fancy wheels, and even the man driving it was black and wearing black from his black dress shoes to his black top hat.

"Are you Mr. Wilson?" He asked; he had a kind face and a cheerful smile.

"Yes," replied Mr. Angel.

"Well, I'm your cab driver."

Mr. Angel climbed on with his bag and helped Aric and Nat on as well.

"Where to sir?" asked the cabdriver when everyone was seated.

"To the nearest cleaner's, and then to a nice inn please," Mr. Angel said.

The cab driver snapped the reins and the horses started trotting along rhythmically.

"What are the horses' names?" Aric asked.

"Why, their names are Droplet and Ripple," said the cab driver proudly.

"How did you come up with those names?" asked Aric.

"They just came to me," said the cab driver, "Hay, do you boys see that old building?"

The cab driver pointed to a building that looked darker than the others, even in the growing morning light. A big dark sign over the door read "Hound Inn" in red letters.

"Yes," said Aric.

"There's an old tale that says a mad man lives in there," said the cab driver.

Nat's attention had been grabbed. Aric started getting a little nervous.

"It also says anyone who enters will become one of his dark-caped slaves," the man gave a cheerful laugh, "but it's just a story."

"Tell us more," Mr. Angel seemed to be getting interested too.

"Well that's about it," said the cab driver.

"Have you seen any caped men around?"

"Well every once and awhile I do, but I doubt they're dark slaves."

"Hmm," Mr. Angel stroked his chin.

When they reached the cleaners the cab driver waited for them outside as they dropped off their dirty clothes. When they came back he took them to the nearest inn.

Before the boys got off the cab driver turned around and handed Nat and Aric each a gold coin.

"You buy yourselves something nice," he said.

"Thank you," said Aric.

"Thanks," said Nat.

"Thank you," said Mr. Angel, "how much do I owe you?"

"Ten silver coins."

Mr. Angel paid the cab driver and helped Nat and Aric down and then followed them with their luggage.

He handed them their backpacks and they waved good-bye to the cab driver and turned toward the inn.

It was obviously Mexican themed. A sign above the door read "Fiesta Hotel". It was a two story building covered in bright colors that were brightened by the morning sun. It looked festive, like a place to have a party.

In fact, as they walked in they heard the sound of people dancing to music and talking and laughing, the air smelled of cheese.

A man at a desk greeted them.

"Hola!" he said, "Welcome to the Fiesta Hotel."

He had a Mexican accent, brown skin and a round face. He had short dark hair and a matching bushy mustache.

"Do you have a three bedroom suite?" asked Mr. Angel.

The man flipped around the pages of a book on the desk.

"No," he finally said, "but, we do have a one bedroom suite with a pull out couch-bed."

Aric was looking around, trying to figure out where the music and party noises were coming from.

"That will work," Mr. Angel agreed.

"How long will you be staying?" asked the deskman.

"I'm not sure, just put us down for a week, we'll cancel if we leave sooner."

The man jotted that down in his book then grabbed a key off a hanger. He handed it to Mr. Angel.

"Room 203," he said with a smile, "feel free to join the party in the fiesta room," he gestured to a big door a little down the hall.

"Thank you, but we have something to deal with first."

Mr. Angel led the boys down the hall towards the spiral staircase.

Aric snuck a peek into the fiesta room and gasped.

"Nat!" Aric said, "Look!"

Amongst the talking, laughing, dancing people was a man in a black cloak. He was definitely one of the Black-Hoods.

Chapter 17
A Plan

"What do we do now?" asked Aric.

The boys sat on the couch watching Mr. Angel pace back and forth while stroking his chin in deep thought.

After Nat and Aric told Mr. Angel that a Black-Hood was in the building, he had raced them up to their room and locked the door.

"We need a plan," Mr. Angel stopped pacing, "and we need one fast, who knows when the Black-Hoods will sneak away with their hostages."

"Why don't we just call the police?" asked Nat.

Mr. Angel shook his head and held his hands behind his back.

"That would be useless without knowing where the Black-Hoods are," he said, "Bork is a big city and the police can't search every nook and cranny of it, at least, not in time. But, I think they might be hiding at Hound Inn."

"Why Hound Inn?" asked Nat.

"Well, that cab driver did say that there are supposed to be men in black clothing around that place," Mr. Angel said.

"He also said that was just a legend," Nat pointed out.

"Well something had to inspire the story," said Mr. Angel, "Besides, it's the only lead we have."

"Well let's tell the police to check Hound Inn," Nat said.

"No, we have to be sure before we alert the authorities. We'll investigate it ourselves tonight."

"What?!" Aric exclaimed, "But what if they catch us?!"

Mr. Angel didn't appear to be listening. Aric didn't argue anymore, he could tell Mr. Angel wasn't going to give up on his idea, no matter what.

"I'm going to go get some supplies we might need for tonight, you two stay here and don't let anyone in except me, here, take the key, I'll get another one from the man at the desk. Got that?"

"Yes," Nat and Aric said.

"If you get hungry you can charge room service to this room, but make sure the man leaves it outside and get it quickly. Ok?"

"Ok," The boys said.

"Lock the door after I leave."

Mr. Angel left and Nat locked the door behind him.

After a short while Nat and Aric got hungry, Nat suggested halving the last pair-apple instead of ordering room service, but even after that, they were still hungry so they ordered two plates of bacon and eggs with a glass of apple juice for Aric and grape for Nat.

Mr. Angel still hadn't returned after the meal so Nat sat down on the couch to read "Journeys" and Aric played Solitaire with some playing cards he'd found in the cabinets.

Mr. Angel returned to find Nat and Aric playing a game of checkers. He showed them the stuff he had bought. Flashlights, rope, a map of that part of Bork, and a big green backpack to keep it all in. He let Nat add in his knife, it might come in handy.

"You two might want to take a nap," said Mr. Angel as he bagged all the stuff back into the backpack, "we'll be staying up late tonight."

Chapter 18
Bork in the Late Night

Bork wasn't too scary at night, it wasn't very dark either. Even though it was the middle of the night, the city was lit up with bright streetlights and store windows that were open late.

The city seemed extra crowded at night. People walked to and fro into stores and restaurants. Some people were talking on the side of the street or at a table in an outdoor cafe surrounded by the smell of fresh bread. Salesmen and women were standing at carts calling out prices or showing someone their merchandise.

Aric loved busy cities, there was so much to see and do. He and Nat looked all around while following Mr. Angel, stopping once or twice to read his map or ask directions to make sure they were headed for Hound Inn.

"I'm pretty sure we're in a big outlet mall," Aric told Nat, "they're always busy in big cities."

After a little more walking Mr. Angel spotted a small costume shop.

"I got an idea," he said.

Mr. Angel gestured for the boys to follow him into the store. Inside a bell on the door greeted them. The man at the counter looked up from his newspaper and said "Hello."

Mr. Angel said "Hello" back and started looking through the racks and shelves.

"What are we doing here?" Nat asked.

"We're going to need camouflage," Mr. Angel whispered so the man at the desk wouldn't hear, "You two find a dark cape or something, a mask might help too."

The boys looked through the mix-mash of faux fur coats, mardi gra masks, clown wigs, and wooden pirate swords until they both found some good camouflage. Nat got a hooded grim reaper robe. The extra strips of fabric hanging off the arms and the fact that it was so long it went past his feet were just troublesome, but Nat had a plan to fix that.

Aric found a vampire's cape and a black fedora.

Mr. Angel found a black hooded cape, almost exactly like the Black-Hoods wear, and black eye masks for all three of them.

Mr. Angel bought the costumes and stuffed them into his backpack. Outside the store he checked the map one more time then led the boys down the street.

As they neared Hound Inn the open shops and carts started to disappear, along with the people. The outlet's white streetlights turned into dim, yellow lights. Eventually, dark apartment buildings and old hotels had replaced all the shops.

"Ok," Mr. Angel stopped and faced the boys, "we need to be very quiet when we get to the Hound Inn, if the Black-Hoods are really in there we don't want to be caught. Got it?"

Nat and Aric nodded.

"Good," Mr. Angel continued walking down the dim street.

Aric found the dimness a little creepy, Nat was scared too, but he knew it was good for it to be dark since they needed to stay hidden.

After turning a corner, Hound Inn came into view. It seemed much darker than the rest of the buildings; you couldn't even make out the red H and O on the rotting sign.

"Come on," Mr. Angel whispered, he pulled the boys back around the corner and into an alley.

The alley was narrow, the walls that made it were crumbly with one or two fading posters hanging loosely from them, a yellow streetlight made the place look ancient.

Mr. Angel took off his backpack and kneeled on the ground.

"Time to put on our camouflage," he said.

He gave Aric his fedora, cape and mask. Nat took his robe and used the knife to cut off the extra fabric and to shorten it at the bottom, they weren't the cleanest cuts and they left frizzles of thread hanging off, but it worked.

Mr. Angel gave Nat his mask and took his own cape and mask.

Now that everyone was in disguise, they snuck around the corner staying close to the walls of the buildings.

Aric felt his fear growing inside him like weeds.

"Look," Mr. Angel pointed to a window on the second floor of Hound Inn.

A dark figure of a man stood in the window.

"I'm pretty sure they're here," Mr. Angel whispered, "That must be a lookout, let's try sneaking around the back."

The boys reluctantly followed Mr. Angel down another alley to an overgrown garden behind the building. Mr. Angel scanned the windows.

"No lookout that I can see," he said, "we'll climb up that ladder to the roof, I bet there's a way in from up there."

Mr. Angel, Nat, and Aric all slowly crept up the splintery latter propped up against Hound Inn.

Aric wondered if he had an undiscovered fear of heights. He looked down. Yes, he was scared of heights. He hoped the old latter could hold all of them.

One by one they crawled onto the roof. It was covered in big crates like the captain's cargo ship. Tube chimneys popped up here and there. A faded redwood door led down into the building.

"We're not actually going down there are we?" Aric asked nervously, he didn't think they'd go this far.

"You two aren't," Mr. Angel said, "but I am. You two stay up here, hide if anyone but me comes up and if I'm not back in a few minutes you sneak away and get the police. Got it?"

Aric and Nat nodded their heads.

As soon as Mr. Angel had snuck through the door, Aric started looking for a hiding place.

"Let's hide in that crate," Aric pointed to a big crate marked "Bananas".

"Ok," Nat said, he and Aric went over to the crate.

Nat gave Aric a leg up and climbed up with Aric's help. They sat on the pile of bananas, squishing a bunch, and waited, hoping the only person to come through the door would be Mr. Angel.

Mr. Angel crept down the creaky, curved stairway. The place reeked of mildew.

He got to the bottom and snuck down a hallway, he heard voices coming from the other side of a door, he gently put his ear up to the moldy wood.

"Are the prisoners all at the clocktower?" a raspy voice asked.

"Yes, sir," said a timid voice.

"Is everything set for tomorrow?"

"Yes, sir."

"What about the ship? Is it ready?"

"Uh, no, sir."

"What?!" yelled the first voice.

"Bu-but it'll be ready by tomorrow," stammered the second voice.

"Good!"

Mr. Angel continued listening; it was very lucky that he caught this conversation.

"I think someone's coming," Aric said.

The boys looked out through the cracks in the crate. The door opened and a man wearing all black, including a black cape, came out.

The Black-Hood took a deep breath, happy to breath in something besides mildew. He sat himself on one of the smaller crates. If Mr. Angel came up now, the kidnapper would definitely see him.

Mr. Angel made his way up the stairs, he had heard more than enough.

He opened the door, just a crack to see if anyone was on the roof... a little more... a little more. He didn't even see the boys, he started getting worried.

"Boys?" he said in a shrill whisper.

"Here," Nat poked his head out of the banana crate.

Mr. Angel walked over, "Did anyone come up?" he asked.

"Yes," Nat said.

Aric poked his head up too, "But he left before you came up."

"Good," Mr. Angel said, "It's smart of you to hide in the crates."

Mr. Angel helped the boys out of the crate and they went back down the ladder and back to the street. When they turned the corner, Mr. Angel told the boys his new plan.

"I overheard them say that your friends are at the clocktower."

"Really?" said Aric, "that's great, we can get the police and-"

"We're not getting the police yet," Mr. Angel said, "we need to go to the clocktower and investigate ourselves first."

"Tonight?" Aric asked, he was already pretty tired.

"Yes," Mr. Angel said.

"Why can't we just get the police if you know where they are?" asked Nat.

"The clocktower might just have been code for another place, we need to make sure before we get the police."

"But why tonight?" asked Aric.

"Because tomorrow will be too late."

The old, victorian clocktower wasn't much more inviting than Hound Inn. A staircase wound up it and it's face needed washing. It sat in the middle of a very small park.

Twelve slow bells sounded. Midnight.

From a distance Mr. Angel and the boys studied the clocktower.

"If they really are in there, there's going to be a guard at the door," Mr. Angel said, "our best bet is to go up those stairs."

Aric gulped. Those stairs looked rickety. His newfound fear of heights wasn't going to help.

Mr. Angel led the way to the stairs and started up. Aric clutched the rail tightly.

About three floors up they reached a window.

"Look," said Nat.

The three of them looked in. Below them was a big cage guarded by a Black-Hood. In the cage were Samuel, Gus, Cynthia, and a few other kids, some of them Nat and Aric recognized and some they didn't.

Samuel was looking fearless as usual. Gus didn't look quite as brave. Cynthia was sitting down crying while one of the braver girls was trying to cheer her up. It made Nat and Aric both angry.

"Ok," Mr. Angel said, "Now we know they're here. Now we get the police."

Aric felt extremely relieved.

They all started down the stairs, ready to get the police.

But at the bottom, they were shocked to find a man in a black cape and mask standing right in their way.

A Black-Hood!

Chapter 19
Logan

"What are you doing here?" the Black-Hood demanded, "You three aren't Black-Hoods."

Mr. Angel didn't even know what to say.

The Black-Hood looked around as if he was about to tell a friend a dark secret.

"They'll catch you if they see you," he whispered.

"Wait, you mean you're not going to get us?" asked Nat.

"Shh!" hissed the man, "Kidnapping isn't exactly my first choice as a career kid, and it's not exactly a job you can quit easily."

"You mean you don't like kidnapping?" Mr. Angel asked.

"Nope," said the man, "never did, I thought joining them would be a good way to stop them somehow from the inside, but I never found a way."

Aric got an idea.

"We're trying to stop them too!" he said, "Can you help us?"

"Um, Aric-" Mr. Angel started.

"Well," said he man, "I do have this," he took out a roll of paper from his cape, "It's a map with the route we're taking the kids tomorrow, I would have taken it to the authorities myself, but our leader gets suspicious if anyone's gone longer than ten minutes."

Aric took the map and handed it to Mr. Angel, who unrolled it and started studying it.

"What time are you leaving?" Aric asked.

"Sunrise," said the man, "now go tell the police about it and get out of here, I've been gone too long now."

He started walking back toward the entrance to the clocktower.

"Wait! One more thing," said Aric, "what's your name?"

"Logan," he answered as he kept going.

"Thanks Mr. Logan," Aric said.

"Come on," Mr. Angel said, rolling the map back up, "we need to get this information to the police."

Mr. Angel, Aric, and Nat had taken off their masks and capes and hats and were now at the police station.

"Ok," said the cop at the front desk, "I'll show this map to the other cops and we'll have an ambush ready for them as they come by tomorrow."

"They also have hideouts at Hound Inn and the Clocktower," Mr. Angel said.

"I'll make sure those places are investigated thoroughly."

"Also, the man who's with them named Logan is the one who gave us the map," added Aric.

"Well," said the cop, "if we catch them we'll make sure he doesn't get arrested."

"Come on," said Mr. Angel, "you two need some sleep."

Outside Nat asked, "Are we going to be there to see them get caught?"

"Of course we will," Mr. Angel said.

"But what if they recognize me and Nat?" asked Aric.

"Hmm," Mr. Angel rubbed his chin in thought, "I have an idea," he said.

Chapter 20
The Escape

The sun wasn't up yet, but it's light was quickly filling shadows everywhere.

Nat, Aric, and Mr. Angel were all standing at the corner of an intersection where the Black-Hoods would be passing any second.

Police hid behind the corners, ready to ambush the kidnappers.

As a disguise, Aric wore his fedora and a pair of reading glasses Mr. Angel had bought him, he couldn't see real well with them but he could make out the blurred figures.

Nat wore a gray hooded coat, not much of a disguise, but then again, the Black-Hoods had only seen them in the dark of night.

Nat stared into the window of the art shop they stood next to. Paint brushes, colored pencils, blank canvases in hundreds of shapes and sizes, and works of art talented artists had chose to sell. Nat envied that talent.

Nat chewed on a stick of gum he had bought with the quarter the cab driver had given him. Aric had used his to buy the hard candy he now sucked on, but didn't satisfy his urge for some breakfast.

"Here they come," Mr. Angel said, "pretend to be looking in the store."

Mr. Angel and Aric joined Nat at staring into the art store's window. Nat turned his head just enough to see a black covered waggon being driven by a black horse steered by a man in a black cape coming their way.

As it came closer three policemen stepped in its way.

"Excuse me sir," the first policeman said to the driver, "in order to pass here you must answer some questions."

The policeman was short and fat but he had a strong, firm voice.

Aric wished the police could just arrest them, but it was illegal to do that without proof they did something wrong. Mr. Angel had explained that to them the night before.

Nat strained to keep himself from looking over at the kidnapper so much. He had thought that the Black-Hood would start acting nervous when the police questioned him, but instead he acted very normal.

"Ok," said the kidnapper.

The policemen started asking questions.

"Hey!" Aric heard someone whisper.

Aric turned around. Out of the back of the waggon Logan stuck out his head, He gestured for them to come over.

Aric nudged Nat and pointed, Mr. Angel saw him too. The three of them casually walked over to Logan, who pulled back the black cover to show Samuel, Cynthia, Gus, and a bunch of other kids that had been kidnapped by the Black-Hoods.

Mr. Angel, Aric, and Nat helped Logan untie and ungag the other kids. Logan and Mr. Angel then brought them all around to the police.

"Excuse me, officer," said Logan, "but I think these kids are what you're looking for."

The Black-Hood in the driver's seat was too flabbergasted at Logan's betrayal to speak.

The policeman smiled and nodded, "Come down from there sir," he said to the kidnapper, "you're under arrest."

After they had taken the kidnapper away, the police sent some cops to investigate the clocktower and Hound Inn.

As Nat, Aric, and their friends had a quick reunion, the few remaining cops and Mr. Angel discussed what to do with the kidnapped kids.

"You'll make sure that they're all back to the places they belong right?" Mr. Angel asked the policeman.

"Yes, sir," He answered, "we'll take great care that these kids are back to their home towns by next week."

"Do you mind if I take Aric, Nat, and their friends home myself?" Mr. Angel asked.

"I don't see why not, Wilson."

"Thank you," Mr. Angel said, "also, what are you going to do with Mr. Logan?"

"Well, I guess he's proven himself a good citizen so I don't suppose prison is fitting."

"Ok, thank you sir."

The police escorted the kids, except for Nat, Aric, Samuel, Gus, and Cynthia, back to the police station.

Nat introduced their friends to Mr. Angel, after that Mr. Angel said, "Well, now I need to rent a horse and waggon to take you kids back in. Let's go to the hotel and let you kids rest while I do that."

Logan came up to them before they left, "Hay, can I come with you?" he asked, "Bork is nice, but it's way too busy for me."

Mr. Angel looked at the kids. Nat shrugged.

"I don't see why not," Mr. Angel said.

Aric and Nat sat in the hotel room telling their friends all about their adventure and their friends, mostly Samuel and Gus, told all about theirs.

Mr. Angel and Logan went out to rent a horse and waggon, buy a map, and gather directions.

Nat, Aric, Samuel, Gus, and Cynthia were still telling stories as they rode in the back of the waggon.

"So, what happened when Ms. Sandyweather found out you were gone?" Samuel asked.

"We don't know," Nat answered.

"We didn't stick around to find out," said Aric.

"Do you think we'll see the hermit on the way home?" Gus asked.

"I hope not!" Aric exclaimed.

Mr. Angel and Logan sat at the front of the waggon, Mr. Angel was steering the horse while Logan studied the map.

"Should I turn right or left at the fork?" Mr. Angel asked.

"Right, through the woods, it's faster," Logan said.

The travelers turned right and, for the second time, Nat and Aric entered the sea of trees.

Chapter 21
Home

Nat and Aric continued their way home on the dirt roads of Nesserad. Their coats protected them from the cold December air.

Aric looked around happily at the falling snowflakes, he actually preferred warm weather, but snow always made the bitter cold worth it.

It had been almost eight months since Mr. Angel had helped Nat and Aric save their friends. Nat's dad had promised they would go visit him. They would leave today, first day of Christmas break.

Nat carried his painting under his arm. It was a painting of the old well surrounded by overgrown winter grass, he had painted it right before it started to snow.

In his other hand he carried his second place trophy from the art contest that morning.

Nat's dad had bought him a ton of art supplies since Nat became interested in art; it was now his favorite hobby.

His dad had also promised, a little too excitedly, that he would make a point to go on more trips in the future since Nat had become, only a little, interested in travel, starting with this trip.

Nervous as he was Nat wondered about the sights he would see and pictures he would draw of them.

"You should have gotten first place," Aric said, "that guy's painting wasn't nearly as good as yours."

Aric was being his over encouraging self as usual. Nat hadn't thought his first few artworks had been that great, but since Aric had insisted he was good he kept drawing.

That late spring day a week or so after they had returned from Bork, Nat had somehow got his dad to adopt Aric, by now the two brothers knew everything about each other.

Aric was about to pile more praise onto Nat's painting, but Cynthia came running up to them.

"Hey, Aric," she said, "The store has new journals! Do you want to come look at them with me?"

Aric looked at Nat. Nat knew Aric wouldn't go if he didn't want him to, but he also knew Aric liked Cynthia, so did everyone else thanks to a couple not-so-secret admirer notes Aric had given her.

Nat gave a nod and Cynthia and Aric ran off towards the store.

Nat decided that since Aric wasn't with him, he'd take the long way home, passed Will's Weapons.

He didn't go in though; he just looked in the display window.

Nat saw Logan at the counter, showing a double bladed sword to a customer. Logan saw him and gave a wave, Nat would have waved back, but his arms were full.

Logan had turned out to be very knowledgeable about weapons, so Nat had told Will about him and he quickly got the job.

Nat continued his way home, when he got there his dad was loading his bags onto the waggon he bought.

"Hi, Nat," he said, "How did you do at the art contest?"

"I won second place!" Nat held up his trophy.

"Congratulations!" his dad said, "You deserve it! One day you'll have so many trophies and medals you won't know what to do with them!"

"Thanks, dad."

"Where's Aric?"

"He went to look at journals at the store, he'll be back soon."

"Good, because I'm all set and ready to go. Have you two at least finished packing?"

"Yes, sir."

"Well, go get your bags."

"Yes, sir."

Nat ran up to his room that he now shared with Aric. He propped his painting against the bed table between their beds and went over to the display case he and Aric had helped his dad make.

It wasn't very full, but it did hold Nat's shoeboxes of knives and daggers including the one Aric had given him. Nat sat his trophy between that and Aric's first place blue ribbon from the poetry contest.

Nat grabbed his and Aric's travel bags from their beds and headed downstairs.

Outside, Aric and their dad were already in the waggon waiting for him.

As Aric helped Nat with the bags their dad asked, "How do you two feel about making a stop in Bork on our way to Mr. Angel's?"

"That would be great!" Nat said.

"Yah, we can finally get our clothes back from that laundry place," Aric said.

The boys climbed into the front seat next to their dad.

"Ready?" asked their dad.

"Ready!" the boys said excitedly.

He snapped the reins and, for the third time, they entered the unpredictable sea of trees.

About the Author

Wolfie Smoke is a lover of books, werewolves, bright colors, spring (even with bad allergies), animals, and of course writing. He loves learning and hates school, he considers the number 13 to be his lucky number, and he refuses to wear the noose most people call "ties". He lives with his family in Hoover, Alabama.

42365996R00066

Made in the USA
Middletown, DE
19 April 2019